SERVED
Hot

A BEST REVENGE NOVEL

SERVED
Hot

A BEST REVENGE NOVEL

MARIE HARTE

Entangled Publishing, LLC
2614 South Timberline Road
Suite 109
Fort Collins, CO 80525
Visit our website at www.entangledpublishing.com.

Brazen is an imprint of Entangled Publishing, LLC. For more
information on our titles, visit www.brazenbooks.com.

Edited by Noah Chinn
Cover design by Fiona Jayde
Cover art from iStock

Manufactured in the United States of America

First Edition December 2014
Rerelease November 2017

ENTANGLED
BRAZEN

Chapter One

The doorbell rang.

Between blackmail, the threat of a lawsuit, and the throbbing hand she'd been sporting since delivering the smackdown of the century last week, Maya figured she'd earned some relaxation time. Screw her "appointment" with Dex—no way in hell she'd call it a real date. The man could get bent. She and her bathtub had plans.

Frickin' Selena Thorpe. Maya snorted. The woman had been a major pain in the ass back in high school. A snob, a bigot and a bully—not only to Maya, but to her two best friends as well. So after learning Selena had ruined Maya's best friend's relationship all those years ago, causing so much pain… Yeah, she'd tricked the woman into returning to Bend for a little payback—a Maya-sized fist to the nose. So what? The bitch had deserved it.

Maya rubbed her knuckles, not at all sorry. If Dex hadn't interfered, she would have knocked out a few of Selena's teeth too, for shits and grins. And her friends said she had anger issues. She chuckled to herself, reliving Selena's shock and ignoring the fact that she'd narrowly avoided a major lawsuit.

Dumb Dex and his meddling cousin had been good for one thing at least. Her heart raced at thoughts of *other* things Dex would surely be good for, so she hastily focused on her bubble bath.

The doorbell rang again. And again. And again.

She ignored it and eased deeper into her tub, sighing with pleasure.

Thunderous knocking soon followed. Maya gritted her teeth and sank under the water. When she finally needed to breathe, she surfaced to silence. Only the flicker of candlelight, the aroma of jasmine and frothy bubbles caressing her skin teased her senses.

She closed her eyes and smiled, enveloped in an all-too-rare tranquility.

"Damn, you're even sexier covered in suds."

Maya screamed, flailed in the tub and nearly drowned herself.

Big hands slid under her arms to pull her above water. They also grazed her breasts when she tried to sink back down.

"*Hey,*" she sputtered.

"Easy, it's just me. If you'd stop squirming, I wouldn't be touching your…ah…there."

She coughed and sat up, crossing her arms over her chest and praying she hadn't decimated the bubbles guarding the rest of her. "What the *hell* are you doing in here?"

Dexter Black. Her nemesis—as she liked to think of him—raised a brow, and she barely held back from launching herself at him and taking the sexy oaf down. She had to crook her head to see all of him. It still floored her that the geeky dweeb she'd literally looked down on in high school had grown so tall.

And turned out so handsome.

From the scrawny nerd who'd once blackmailed her to be his prom date, Dex had matured into a hot-as-hell infuriating male. With his short black hair, broad chest, and even his big-ass feet, the man put the S in sexy. For the life of her, she couldn't seem to block him from her thoughts.

And lucky, lucky Maya, the guy had recently moved back to Bend. Permanently.

He quirked a grin. "Got room in there for me?"

"Don't you dare move," she ordered. "Why are you in here? *How* did you get in here?"

"You left your door unlocked."

"So you felt it was okay to come on in?"

He narrowed his eyes. "You have a problem with it? Call the cops and have them arrest me for breaking and entering."

She'd like to, but then… "Why? So you can squeal on me to them about Selena? No thanks."

"Exactly." He gave a satisfied smile which faded as he stared at her. "I'm confused. Why are you in the bath? Did you forget we have a date tonight?"

"The first of many," she sneered. "I can't believe you have to blackmail women into going out with you." She really couldn't. At six-four, with dark hair, light gray eyes and a body that now featured in her dreams, the man caused mini-orgasms by simply breathing.

"I only blackmail the really pretty ones." He winked, the bastard.

She had to fight not to smile. Not known for having a great sense of humor, Maya thought it odd that even after twelve years of not seeing him, Dex could still get her to smile.

"Dex…"

"Hey, blame yourself. Who the hell doesn't lock their doors at night?" He frowned at her. "That's not safe."

"I thought I had. I usually do." But she'd been flustered at thoughts of what he might do if she avoided him. She didn't want to go out with Dex, because she did. She was just perverse enough to torture herself by going after unattainable guys. Handsome, rich, funny Dex definitely qualified as above her pay-grade. She'd stick to poor bad boys, thank you very much.

"Maya." He sighed. "What's our deal?"

"You make it sound like this is something we both agreed to. You blackmailed me *again*, you bastard," she muttered, though the fact he'd been underhanded enough to coerce her into a date showed he had promise. Not so good after all.

"Hey, I'm not the one who punched Selena Thorpe in the face. I'm just a helpless witness, who may or may not have a selective memory."

"Helpless, my ass."

He grinned. "And though it goes against my trustworthy and honest nature—" he ignored her snort of derision "—I've agreed to lie for you. That whole 'Selena walked into a door and broke her nose' bit is pretty thin. But for you, I'll say it."

"You're lying for who, exactly?" He wanted a date. Correction. He wanted *ten* dates where they'd go out in public and hold hands. Emotional romantic crap. Maya had better things to do. Or so she kept telling herself.

"I lie for *you*, my lovely victim." He leered, and she coughed to hide a laugh.

"You already fibbed to the cop that asked about Selena's story. Now if you admit to the cops that you lied, you're in trouble too."

"Not according to Selena." His knowing smile irked her, because she knew Selena would do anything but get Dex in trouble. Selena would persuade Dex to come to the dark side. No doubt the skank would make sure she got some quality sack time with him in the bargain. Any heterosexual woman with a pulse would jump the guy.

And that, right there, was a sign for Maya to watch her step. *She* did the seducing. She held the power in her relationships. With Dex, she had a feeling she'd be the one taking commands, not giving them. She clung to her denial. "I still don't think anyone will believe her over me, even if you back her up."

"Yeah, but it won't just be me. It'll be Anson too." His cousin, another prick she and her friends had to deal with now that he'd moved back to town.

"I still don't get it. You're lying for a date. With me." What did Dex really want, apart from annoying her? It had to be sex.

"Not just *a* date. Ten dates."

Shoring up her courage, she plunged in. "Look, why don't we just get this out of the way. We'll screw, then you'll have what you want and I won't be wasting my time with you." Her body sang at the thought of getting Dex under her, but she put on her bored face, trying not to seem too keen on the idea.

He watched her, his gaze moving over what seemed to be every flipping bubble in her bath and ending on her sore hand. "How are those knuckles doing, baby?"

She wanted to show him, fist to nose. Typical of him to ignore what he didn't want to answer. "They're fine, *baby.*"

"Riley said they're bruised and that you can't make any new clay pieces for a while."

"When did you talk to Riley?"

He shrugged, sat on the edge of the tub—*way too close*—and didn't even pretend not to stare at her body. "I went to visit Anson yesterday and stopped next door at her place for a cupcake. That girl can bake like nobody's business."

"Yeah, I know." She had half a loaf of decadent pumpkin bread in her freezer. Just in time for Thanksgiving in a few weeks. That's if she didn't go to jail for killing Dex first.

"So, about your offer..." He trailed a finger in her bathwater and skimmed her knee.

She shot back in the tub, sloshing water and scowling at him. If a simple touch turned her on, she could only imagine what a kiss might do. Oh man. Not good.

"You're scared." His satisfied smile should have irked her. Instead his confidence turned her on even more.

"Excuse me?"

"Yep. Scared of me, which is weird because I'm not out to *bump you and dump you*," he emphasized. Obviously he'd heard all about her friend Ann's failed plan to use and lose his buddy Jack. "I just want to spend some quality time with a beautiful woman who's not all about getting into my pants or my wallet. You don't want to go out with me, and excuse me for being confused, but the last time we talked, you refused to fuck me as payment for keeping my silence. So I'm not too sure why I should think your offer for a quick fuck is on the table now."

She seriously wished he'd stop saying *fuck*, because every time he did he sounded like he was making an offer she'd be stupid to refuse.

She swallowed hard. "I, ah, I'm uncomfortable, okay? I'm naked, you big goon. At least let me get out of the tub so we can have this discussion while I'm dressed."

"No. Answer me now. What's it gonna be? Will you stick by your word or not? I really do hate to resort to blackmail."

She wanted so badly to tell him to shove his dates where the sun didn't shine. But she'd shook hands on their dumb deal. Ten dates and he kept silent about exactly which blunt object had knocked Selena's nose out of joint. Maya never reneged on a promise—a code she'd stood by her entire life. And he knew it.

"Blackmail is such a dirty word. Figures you're the one using it." She glared at him.

He chuckled. "Good thing you're cleaning up then, hmm?" His eyes darkened, as they usually did when he watched her. He wanted her but refused an offer of casual sex? The man made her brain hurt.

She sighed. "I'll go out with you tonight, okay? Now leave the bathroom so I can get dressed."

"Not on my account."

"Dexter Black!"

"Okay, okay." He cringed. "No yelling. Or hitting," he warned. "'Cause you hit me, I'll hit you back."

"Yeah, right." She couldn't see him abusing a woman. Dex had been and still was a gentleman to his toes. She could almost smell that sense of decency on him...which made his blackmail both cute and annoying but not truly threatening.

"There's hitting, and there's *hitting*." He licked his lips, his gaze on her mouth. His sly grin had her backing up even more in the tub. She shivered at the cool air hitting her wet skin. "I'd love to hit that mouth with my own. Lick my way down your body." He lost his smile, and her libido fired up into a bonfire. His stare centered on the vanishing bubbles near her breasts. "Maybe stop to feast on your—"

"I'm getting out," she wheezed, alarmed to have lost control of her vocal cords...and other parts of her body. God, her nipples were hard as rocks. "Move it, Black." Her cheeks felt hot, which made no sense. Maya had no problem sexing it up with men. The more casual the acquaintance, the better. So why the hell did Dex's admiration fluster her so much?

"Fine. But don't blame me for having to get tough. A few dates and all your problems disappear." He shrugged. "No worries about Selena tattling. No having to explain to the Terrible Trio why they have to be Terrible Duo since you're in jail for assault and battery."

She snorted. "You always this chatty with naked women?"

"It's either chatty or we get to fucking. And despite what you said, you seem a little squeamish about having sex on our first date, so I'm willing to wait."

She blinked up at him. "*What?*"

"Unless I misread things, but—"

"Out." She pointed at the door.

He grinned, made a point of looking over her one last time, then stood and sauntered out of the bathroom. He didn't close the door behind him.

• • •

Dex drew in a deep breath and let it out slowly while he waited for Maya in her living room. He'd known she'd throw up roadblocks for their first outing. Granted, it wasn't as if he'd earned her compliance in a morally decent kind of way. Being forced to blackmail a woman into going out with him should have hurt his pride, but that he'd out-maneuvered Maya satisfied him on a deeper level. He might annoy or anger her, but at least he didn't bore her.

Maya Werner was the one who got away. Back when he'd been smaller and kind of, well, nerdy, he'd been love-struck by the statuesque beauty. She was nearly six feet tall, had long dark hair and coppery skin that seemed to glow. A natural beauty with sex appeal, even at seventeen, she'd been one of the most talked-about girls back in high school. Though the talk wasn't always positive.

Some of the guys had called her stuck-up or made fun of her mixed Native American heritage, while others like Selena had their own petty reasons for snubbing her. Dex had never seen anything but her true beauty. Then he'd had to change high schools for his senior year and feared he'd missed his shot with her. Fast forward to a small bit of trickery and he'd had the best prom ever.

Maya had always been nice to him, even on prom night. She'd laughed and danced with him, enjoying herself around strangers. But the moment they'd run into her peers, she'd changed. Closed up, guarding a heart he suspected had been bruised or broken a long time ago.

Not much had changed in the twelve years since.

Well, other than she'd gotten even more appealing than she'd been in her youth. He wanted her more now than he had then. Not for a quick fuck—and wow, had *that* been difficult to turn down. He focused on stifling his constant erection, which didn't seem to ease when Maya was around.

Rustling in her bedroom reminded him of how naked she'd been just moments ago. The woman looked damn good in bubbles.

He groaned.

"What?" she yelled from the other room.

"Nothing. Just waiting. As usual."

He heard her swear and smiled. Maya hadn't changed much. Still trying to keep everyone away, according to his friends. She rarely dated anyone seriously, preferring carnal and unattached relationships. Casual sex with her would have been amazing, then left him forgotten on her long list of conquests. But Dex didn't intend to be just another name on her list; he planned to be the *last* on her list.

She entered the living room wearing jeans, a loose aqua-blue sweater that exposed a toned shoulder, and her hair down. It had always been pretty straight and in the light appeared blue-black. The woman was fucking gorgeous.

He walked to her side and lifted a piece of her hair off her sweater. She tensed as he brought the hair up and sniffed. "Mmm."

She blushed. "Would you stop? You have no idea what 'personal space' means, do you?"

"Nope." He shoved his hands in his pockets and tried to give himself more room in his jeans. His dick refused to go down. At the words *go down*, he couldn't help envisioning Maya on her knees, her mouth wide open…

"You okay? You look like you're in pain." Maya smirked at him. "We can always cancel tonight if you're not feeling up to snuff." Her telling gaze lingered over his fly.

"I'm just fine." He smiled back, wanting to nibble his way down her body. "Hungry is all."

"I'll bet." She strolled to the hall closet, grabbed her shoes and jacket and finished dressing. "Well?"

"I'm driving." He put a hand on the small of her back to guide her out of her cottage. "Lock up."

"Okay, here's the thing." She locked her door, and the sound of the deadbolt closing relieved him. He hadn't liked that she'd left her door unlocked while taking a bath.

"The thing?"

"I said I'd date you, so I will. You keep your mouth shut about Selena, and I'm your arm candy for a few nights." She stepped close to him and poked him in the chest. "That doesn't mean you get to boss me around. And we already took sex off the table, because I'm not a whore who can be bought with your silence."

"Or bought with anything else?" He laughed when her eyes narrowed. "Teasing. Maya, I never called you a whore or inferred it. I simply want to spend some time with you."

"Whatever. Let's go."

He would have taken more offense at her attitude if he didn't see the small signs of nerves he'd long ago committed to memory. Back in high school, he'd been obsessed with her. The Marine Corps had broadened his perceptions and allowed him to experience life and relationships in far-off lands and with a diverse group of people. Yet nothing about his memories of Maya had faded.

She bit her lower lip, glared at him and stomped her way to his truck. Oh yeah, the woman was nervous, which fascinated him. Maya usually held the world by the balls. He couldn't imagine that in the time he'd been gone, and with her surly demeanor, much had changed since he'd left. When something got under her skin, it meant more to her than a casual interest.

Buoyed by the thought he might just be able to seduce her into his bed and hopefully into his life, he got behind the wheel and drove.

They arrived at a small hole-in-the-wall bar on the south side of town. The place had greasy food, great music and an intimate atmosphere.

"Never been here." Maya stared around her, taking in the biker décor and live rock playing at a non-earsplitting decibel. "This is nice."

"Well, I thought about taking you to the Astro Lounge, but they're all about drinks and banging college girls."

"Yeah, I'm not into college girls anymore."

He blinked, waiting for more and not getting it. "That's all you're saying? You can't leave me hanging, Maya. Did you really go out with a woman?"

"Once. Not my thing, but she was really cute."

He groaned. "You did that on purpose. Now I'll be spending the night thinking about you and some young, nubile chick in bed."

She laughed. "Nubile? Geez. You and Ann should get together and play Scrabble."

"I would, but Jack won't let me get near her."

Maya frowned. "She's happily in love with the guy. Leave her alone."

Yep. Always loyal to her friends. Was it any reason he'd been captivated by her from day one? Gorgeous, funny, smart, loyal, and yet she watched everyone with caution, as if waiting for someone to throw the first punch. Back then, he'd wanted to be the one to protect her. To his bemusement, he still did.

"Dex," she growled. "I mean it."

"Easy, Maya. Ann's cute, but she's not my type." He decided to start his seduction. Slowly, but not so subtly that she wouldn't know what he wanted. The key to Maya was to keep her off balance and interested. "I prefer a woman with a little meat. Some curves. Darker skin, straight black hair…"

"Really? A little meat? My heart's all aflutter."

"You know me. Mr. Charm." He shrugged off his jacket, gratified when Maya gave him a thorough once-over.

"Are you on steroids?"

"No. Eight years in the Marine Corps bulked me up. And trust me, it feels better to be this big in a bar fight than the skinny twerp I was in high school."

She smiled. "You were cute then. Little, but cute." She shook her head then glanced down at the menu on the table. "Too bad you grew up."

He laughed, and his entire being locked up at seeing her mean grin. He could spend hours watching her. But being mesmerized wouldn't win him any points. "Baby, I can handle you with one hand tied behind my back. I'm not the one who was scared to go on a date."

The teasing left her dark eyes. "How's that?"

He shrugged and looked at his own menu. "Just saying, I can go out with a woman, not expect sex, enjoy myself and move on with life. You seem to think every man who sees you wants to do you." They most likely did, but it wouldn't help to stroke the woman's ego. "Or that I might want a date for immoral reasons."

"So you're saying you *don't* want to do me?"

He shrugged. "I could go either way. Sure, you're pretty. But sometimes a guy wants more from a woman." He chanced a look at her.

She didn't appear angry, but fascinated. "Like what?"

The waitress bussed by and took their orders, then left with a warm smile directed at him.

"Hello?" Maya snapped. "I thought you just said you want more from a woman than sex."

"I did. Why are you mad at me?"

"Look, you wanted a date. Stop flirting with the waitress and answer my question."

He bit back a grin. She didn't like that look their cute waitress had given him? Excellent sign. "I wasn't flirting. Smiling is how you win friends and influence people. Take note." He ignored her middle finger. "Anyway, when I decide to date a woman, sure, physical attraction is a key factor. But I need more. I want to like her smile, the way she deals with other people. Is she bitchy or nice? Selfish or giving?"

Maya smirked. "So why are we out then? I'm not nice. And I'm told I'm selfish."

"Nah. You're nice to your friends and the people around you. Just not to men who you're attracted to. Namely—me."

"Dream on." She paused. "So what else?"

"I can take care of myself. I cook and clean. I make a decent living." A lucrative one thanks to his skill behind a camera and the business sense to know how to make smart financial decisions. "I'd expect a woman I'm interested in to be the same."

"What if she can't cook? What if she's a slob? What if she's broke? You seem to want a lot from a woman. A little exacting. Maybe that's why you're still single."

"I could say the same about you."

"Me? I'm simple. I want a man who's good in bed. Maybe we talk while we fuck, maybe we don't." She shrugged, and her dark eyes invited him to stare and keep on staring. "I have my friends for fun. I trust them, they trust me, and we all get along. Riley, Ann and I do everything together."

"Really? So you, Ann, Jack and Riley are sharing the same bed?"

"Okay, not everything. But Jack accepts Ann is part of a

tight group of friends. Just because they're all gooey in love doesn't mean that will change."

Then why do you look so scared? he wanted to ask.

The waitress returned with their food. As the meal progressed and their talk turned to friends he hadn't seen in years, he thought the date had gone amazingly well.

An hour and a half after they'd arrived, Maya pushed her beer away and sighed. "I'm stuffed. What now?"

He gave her a sly smile designed to unnerve her. When she sat up straighter in her chair and frowned, he knew he'd been successful. "Now we go home. And we go to bed."

Chapter Two

"Bed? Are you high? Didn't we talk about this?" Maya tried to ignore the butterflies wrestling in her stomach.

He laughed. "You're so easy. I meant, we go home, where I drop you off. You go to your bed. Then I go home to mine."

Bummer. "Good. For a second there I thought you'd forgotten the rules."

His smile aggravated her, because he seemed to be laughing at some joke she wasn't in on.

They left the restaurant after he took care of the bill. She didn't even try to offer to pay, since this whole thing had been his idea.

As they drove back to her house in his truck, she had to admit she'd enjoyed herself. One thing she could say for Dex, he never lost her interest. Even as a kid he'd been witty. A smart guy who didn't try to trade on his looks or money. Many of the kids she'd gone to school with had come from wealth and had no problem sharing that fact. Dex had never traded on his family's connections, using his own work ethic and intellect to get ahead.

She respected him for that, but she still couldn't get past the fact he'd gotten the better of her *again*. Especially since she was supposed to be winning their little contest of wills.

Only a few weeks ago she'd gathered with her girlfriends over wine, each determined to set things right with those who had done them wrong. Her grudge was with Dex. Ann had dealt with Jack, and Riley was still handling Anson—kind of. Maya needed to talk to the levelheaded member of their group. At least Ann had made Jack work to earn her devotion. Maya planned to kick Dex's ass…somehow. Just as soon as this stupid bet ended. But Riley seemed to be floundering with Anson. Probably because she was too nice.

Not like Maya.

She turned and noted Dex watching her out of the corner of his eye.

"Answer me this," she ordered.

He saluted. "Yes, ma'am."

"You graduate high school, spent—how many years in the Marine Corps?"

"Eight."

"Right. Eight. Then you left to become some big-name photographer."

"Photojournalist."

"Whatever. You're successful and getting paid big money. So you leave all that and come back to Bend. Why?"

"Why not?" He drove with easy competence. The jerk did everything well. Which made her wonder what he'd be like between the sheets… "My family is here. I've been all around the world. Well, to most of the places I wanted to visit anyway. I'm ready to set down roots, and I love my hometown." He paused. "You're still here. You must love Bend."

"I do." She loved the mountains, the dry weather, the glorious snow and her lovely fireplace that kept her warm during the cold. "Dad is here. My friends are here. I get loving this town. But you left and then came back, and practically the first thing you do is blackmail me again? What, is this how you get all your dates?"

He grinned and pulled into her driveway. He didn't turn off the truck but put it into park and turned to face her. "You're still hung up on what happened twelve years ago, aren't you?"

She fumed. "Yes, damn it. Because the only way you could have gotten that picture of me pranking the principal was if you'd been stalking me."

"I prefer the term *reconnaissance*. I was watching you, trying to get up the nerve to ask you to pose for me. I've always liked photography, remember?"

"Yeah. But—"

"So imagine my surprise when my muse darted into her high school's main office, set off two cans of silly string, then painted a mustache over a picture of Principal Weber. Funny? Yes. Worth my time and effort to capture you on film? Hell, yeah. And it paid off. I had the hottest date at the prom."

She narrowed her eyes. "That smile does not say 'I'm sorry.' The fact you're blackmailing me now proves it. You should be ashamed of yourself."

"Whatever." He scooted closer, and she tensed. "Come here."

"No."

He sighed and turned off the truck. "I can sit here all night."

Figuring he might, she relented. Better for her to be rid of him and tamp down the desire plaguing her. "Fine." She moved an inch closer, wishing the stupid truck had bucket seats.

"Not close enough." He yanked her until their thighs welded, then turned her face and kissed her.

She would have pulled back, but his hand fisted in her hair, and the small tug he gave eroded any resistance. She became clay under his artful hands as he held her while his mouth did wicked things to her.

The taste of him—dark beer and heady man—made her drunk with desire. She'd never responded so readily for anyone as Dex kissed his way under her skin. His tongue tangled with hers, pulling a sigh out of her.

Unable to help herself, she moaned and clutched his shirt, more than aware of the firm muscles beneath it. Her breasts tingled and her entire body ached for more of his touch. Any minute now and she expected to feel those large hands on her breasts, moving slowly down her belly to her jeans and below...

He pulled back, breathing hard. His eyes had gone beyond smoky to thunderous slits of slate gray. "That's how you end a date."

He moved like lightning, one minute so close to her they shared breaths, the next out of the truck and pulling her with him. He left her at her front door. "Lock up this time, okay?" He stood there, waiting.

With a shaky hand, she found her key and let herself inside, locking up behind her. Moments later she heard the rumble of his truck leaving. Then she stumbled to her couch and melted into it, wondering what the hell had just happened.

She wiped her mouth but couldn't take the taste of Dex from her lips. She didn't understand how she'd gone from enjoying dinner with him, arguing, talking, laughing, to discussing his extortion of her in the truck. Instead of becoming angry, she'd been confused and aroused and let him tug her into the best kiss she'd had in... Hell, *ever*.

Even worse, after kissing her senseless he'd dumped her at her front door with a smile, leaving her frustrated and needy. He'd been totally in control while she trembled and moved in a fog.

"Jesus, the man can kiss." And she had nine more dates with him, nine more times to be tempted to jump him, lose face, and become another notch on his belt. How the hell would that end her fixation—*need for closure*—with the man?

Maya had trouble sleeping. She knew she needed to come up with a better plan for dealing with Dex, yet she couldn't think of one. *She* couldn't, but she had a feeling Riley or Ann might be able to help.

• • •

Saturday morning, she called for reinforcements. They met for lunch at Riley's place. Maya would have preferred breakfast, but Ann would need time to break away from Jack. The lucky girl was still hot and heavy with the guy she loved. Maya wasn't totally heartless. She'd let Jack have Ann for the morning.

Sitting with Riley in the kitchen and helping her best friend fix sandwiches, she asked what she'd been dying to know. "So how are things with Anson?"

Riley frowned. Frowning, laughing, or crying, Riley Hewitt was still the most beautiful woman Maya had ever seen. Far from being a bitch about it, Riley acted as if she had no clue how people reacted to her. With cocoa brown skin, hazel eyes, and thick brown hair she normally wore in a ponytail, the woman always looked as if she'd just stepped off a magazine cover.

Yet Riley acted baffled when complimented on her looks. Maya often wondered how she could be so clueless.

When Riley continued to frown and started to pound the cookie dough she'd been playing with, Maya sighed. "Hello? Earth to Riley. Stop daydreaming about Anson and tell me what's going on."

"Daydreaming? Yeah, right." Riley glared at the cookie dough and started rolling small balls onto a baking sheet. "That bastard is on my last friggin' nerve. Do you know he had the audacity to send his guys over to my place to eat?"

"Um, you own a bakery. That's why people come by, right?"

"Don't be deliberately dense. Anson is renovating right next door, creating a restaurant that will take away from my business. And he has the nerve to send those men helping to run me out of business by for cupcakes!"

Maya shrugged. "So don't serve them."

"I can't do that." Riley looked aghast. "They're paying customers. Some of them are pretty nice guys. It's not their fault they work for a jerk."

"I don't understand you."

"I thought I was pretty clear."

Maya rolled her eyes. "For someone so smart and successful, you're kind of stupid."

"Said the pot to the kettle," Riley grumbled and finished with the cookies. She put the tray in the oven and stared at the sandwiches Maya had been making. "What exactly are you doing to my ham and cheese?"

"What you told me to do."

Riley took the food away from Maya and redid the sandwiches, adding mustard, some cranberry chutney and avocado.

Maya's mouth watered. "I'm *so* hungry."

"We're waiting for Ann."

"Oh, come on. She's busy getting busy with Jack. Ha. Busy getting busy. Get it?"

Riley gave a half grin. "I'll tell her you said that."

"Good. And while you're at it, explain to her how you and Anson are competing with each other, because I don't get it. I mean, I know you guys have been rivals since that science fair—when was that?"

"Third grade," Riley muttered.

"Jesus. That far back?" Maya sighed. "And I thought I held a grudge. Look, when I thought he was starting a bakery right next door to yours, I was livid. Now, knowing it's an actual restaurant? You guys could co-exist." Seeing Riley's grimace, she amended, "Co-exist in mutual dislike, I mean. Oh hell, forget I said that. What was I thinking to advocate communal happiness?"

"Yeah. What were you thinking?"

"Go doctor up a cupcake. Put something in it to give him the runs. Then manage a way to get his guys to give it to him so it doesn't seem like you're in on it."

"Now you're just being silly."

And ridiculous, but Maya grinned. "Admit you're thinking about it."

"No comment." The doorbell rang, and Riley blew out a breath. "Thank God. Someone with common sense has arrived."

Ann entered with the glow of someone in love. A natural redhead with big blue eyes and a petite frame someone as tall as Maya envied, Ann had a generous heart and a loving nature. Ms. Too Nice, Maya liked to call her. Hell, the woman even taught elementary school kids. It was like she was trying to win a gold medal in Olympic sweetness.

"And we're finally complete. The Terrible Trio rides again." Maya held up a ham and cheese, stuck her tongue out at Riley and bit into the sandwich.

They all gathered at the kitchen island, where Maya and Ann sat as Riley continued to fuss around the kitchen. "I made her wait for you," Riley explained to Ann. "She was whining like crazy."

"I'm hungry and my head hurt from trying to understand how you're having so much trouble with Anson," Maya said around her food.

"Would you please chew, swallow *then* talk?" Riley grimaced. "Gross."

Maya opened her mouth, which was full of food, wider, and Riley groaned.

Ann laughed. "I missed you guys. It's been all of what, four days? Yet nothing seems to have changed since I've been with Jack."

"Yep," Riley agreed. "Maya is still a huge pain in my ass."

"All I hear is blah, blah, blah. Pass the lemonade." Maya joined in their humor, though a good part of her remained cautious. Ann had finally snagged the love of her life. It was only a matter of time before she started pulling away from the group. Date nights with Jack that interfered in wine nights with the girls. She and Jack would get married, have kids. Possibly move out of town if Jack's job took them away, breaking up their trio...

Riley snapped her fingers in front of Maya's face. "Hey, dream girl. Wake up. Ann asked you a question."

Maya swallowed her food past a dry throat. "Huh?"

"So eloquent." Ann snorted. "Pass me a sandwich and tell me how your date with Dex went."

Riley lit up. "Oh yeah. I totally forgot that was last night. Funny you didn't mention it."

"I was going to tell you." Maya hoped her cheeks didn't look as warm as they felt.

"So? How did it go?" Riley grabbed a sandwich. "Is he groveling at your feet yet?"

Ann smiled. "I think it's cute he pretended to blackmail you into dating him."

"Pretended? The bully said he'd go to the cops." Yet Maya knew he wouldn't.

"Please." Riley huffed. "He never liked Selena Thorpe. Remember? He wasn't one of the in-crowd back in high school. Like us, well, like you and me, he was an outsider."

Ann shook her head. "I might have been a little popular, but you forget the star quarterback broke my heart in front of the entire senior class. I lost any popularity I had."

"Technically you lost that in second grade when we became best friends," Maya countered. "Hang with the outcasts and you can't help but get some dirt on you."

"Good point." Riley grinned, losing the tension she'd been carrying earlier.

"You two had tons of friends. You just like to think you didn't because it's more dramatic." Ann pointed at Maya. "You, especially, can be a real drama queen."

"Yes, she can." Riley checked on the cookies, then returned to the island. "And don't think all this chatter has distracted us from the date you still haven't described. Talk, sister."

Maya groaned. "It was horrible." She recounted everything, from the scare in the tub to the scorching kiss in the truck. "How the hell do I one-up him if I'm always thinking about doing him?" She glared at Ann. "And get that stupid, sappy look off your face. This ain't hearts and flowers here, kid. My body might want him, but the man bugs me. He *still* hasn't said he's sorry for forcing me to go out with him."

"You talking about the prom, or your recent date where he not only paid, he kissed you senseless afterward?" Riley asked, overly polite.

"Shut up. At least I have a reason to be wary around Dex. You can't even find a real reason to dislike Anson."

"Other than that he's a dick," Riley said.

"Well, yeah, there is that," Maya admitted, wishing she didn't sound so pathetic. If only Dex would be more of an asshole, then she'd be able to be firmer in her stance to reject and hate him. The sexy jerk made it difficult to hold onto her grudge, and Maya had a reputation as a champion grudge-holder.

She ran a hand through her hair, feeling the need to pull it out strand by strand. "Why are we talking about Riley and Anson anyway? You guys are supposed to be helping *me*."

Riley scowled. "Look, dumbass, *you're* the one who brought up Anson. Not me."

"It's called avoidance," Ann said. "Maya doesn't want to admit that she actually likes Dex and always has." She turned to Maya. "Let's be honest. Of the three of us, you've got the easygoing adversary. I had a real beef with Jack. Hello? Pregnancy scare? He dumped me in public? And Riley has always been competing with Anson. We all agree he's conceited."

"Yeah." Riley planted her hands on her hips, nodding.

Maya took another bite of her sandwich, never too emotionally compromised to eat. After chewing and swallowing—to satisfy the prissy Miss Manners—she said, "I don't know that I'd call Dex easy, but I agree with you about Jack and Anson."

"Dex is such a nice guy. I always liked him."

"I don't do nice."

Riley smirked. "Funny. Seems to me you *want* to."

After giving her friend the finger, which Riley happily returned, Maya groaned. "Look, you two, I have nine more dates with the guy. Yeah, I want to have sex with him. He didn't take me up on my first offer, but I think he wants me. I mean, I *know* he wants me." As much as she wanted him? Damn it. She wished she knew him better.

"He did kiss you in the truck." Riley looked thoughtful. "Maybe he ended the kiss so suddenly so he wouldn't jump your bones. You know he's always liked you. It follows if he wants to date and not sleep with you right away that he's a sincere kind of guy. I think it's sweet."

Maya hated sweet. "That's the problem. I don't like nice

or sweet. And don't even describe the guy as kind." She shuddered. Give her a bad boy any day.

"But you want him." Ann narrowed her eyes. "I say go after him. Don't make this about trying to get even or making him apologize for prom night. You want him? Be your take-charge self and grab him. You and Dex get some hot sex, you have some fun, and maybe you part as friends. Everybody's happy. What's not to like about that?"

Riley agreed. "And if you're too stubborn to take on that hunk of man, let me know. Because he is right up my alley. I love nice."

Maya glared. "You're so full of it." The idea of Riley going after Dex bothered Maya. A lot. They'd never poached on one another's guys before. Not that Dex belonged to Maya or anything, but—

"You see that, Ann?"

"Yep."

Maya didn't know what they were talking about. "What?"

"You get that line between your brows when you're really annoyed." Riley's smug smile aggravated Maya all over again. "You don't like the thought of me anywhere near Dex. You don't just lust after him. You *like* him. Admit it."

"What is this, second grade?" She sneered at Riley, then Ann—a second grade teacher.

"Oh yeah." Ann laughed at her. "You pegged it, Riley. Maya has the hots for Dex. Lighten up, Maya. Follow my advice. I did what you told me to do with Jack, and look at me now. I'm in *looovvee.*"

"Ew." Maya tried to be angry but couldn't hold out against Ann's dopey smile. "Yeah, but if you remember, my advice was to be mean. To bump and dump him." She heard an echo of Dex's deep voice in her memory. "Your advice is for me to play nice with the enemy."

Riley took the cookies out of the oven and gave Maya a

look—the one that said, *you're so full of it.* "Dex isn't anyone's enemy. He's a great guy with a terrific sense of humor. If you'd stop being so stubborn, you'd realize you liked him back then, and you like him even more now."

Maya stared at her best friends, struggling with her inner bitch as well as her inner artiste. Angst made for a hell of a creative bent, but it was exhausting. Trying to hate Dex took too much energy, and lying to herself about how she felt was harder than it should have been.

She sighed. "Hell. I do like him." It galled her to say, but she couldn't ignore the truth. "So what? Fuck him and then we go our separate ways?"

"Crass, but why not?" Ann shrugged. "You're both consenting adults. Dex wants to date you, so he obviously likes you. Why not enjoy time with the man, have some killer sex—because just looking at Dex makes you think the man is a god in bed—and still be friends? Not all guys are out to shaft you, Maya."

Riley snickered. "To hear Maya tell it, they're *all* about shafting her."

Maya laughed with her. "I wouldn't mind *shafting* Dex." Boy was that the truth.

"Oh stop." Ann sighed. "What am I going to do with you two?" Then she started laughing with them.

Maya made a memory of the moment—watching her friends, feeling warmth and acceptance from head to toe. Her friends had always been there for her. A family when she only had her father for comfort. Sisters of her heart and a never-ending source of camaraderie, love and laughter.

Three things she'd never been able to get from any man not her father, unfortunately. She didn't need a man, not when she had a real family.

So why did a sudden image of Dex's smiling eyes continue to plague her with promises of an impossibility?

Chapter Three

Saturday night, Dex had managed to pry Jack away from Ann and hung out with Anson at their favorite bar downtown. A nice hole-in-the-wall that served cheap beer on draft, decent scotch for the price and catered more to the late twenties/ early thirties crowd than to the college kids at the bar next door.

"So." Anson took a large drag on his beer.

"Nice to see you out from under a hard hat." Dex grinned at his cousin.

They looked enough alike that people often thought them brothers. Both had dark hair, large builds and similar features—square jaws, a stubborn nose, long-lashed eyes. But Dex had pretty gray eyes, not the ugly green ones Anson always bragged about. Dex also wore his hair military short, while Anson preferred his to drop down his neck.

He stared at Anson's hair. "Too long, you friggin' hippy."

Anson smirked at him and flipped his hair, causing Jack to grin.

"I'm so glad you guys moved back. What perfect timing."

Jack clinked his beer against their glasses. "It's hard being the only guy around the Terrible Trio. I worry about getting overloaded with estrogen." He laughed.

Dex laughed with him. Everyone knew how over-the-moon happy he was with his old high school sweetheart Ann. Though Jack, like Dex and Anson, had been out of town since graduating, they'd all managed to move back in time to rekindle old friendships—and old flames.

Speaking of which… "I blackmailed Maya into dating me."

Anson rolled his eyes. "And you wonder why I don't tell people we're related."

Jack snorted. "You think that's smart? Woman will slit your throat while you sleep, and we'll be lucky to find your body. You know she has a kiln."

"Right. The artist." Maya crafted amazing pottery and had been showcased in galleries across the Northwest. Sexy, gorgeous and skilled. Was it any wonder he still had the hots for her?

"So how was the date?" Jack asked.

"Really? We're going to gossip about a girl like, well, *girls*?" Anson sneered.

"I already filled him in," Dex explained to Jack. Dex and Anson lived together in a nice rental on the West side. For all that Anson acted like an arrogant ass most of the time, he hid a heart of gold. The only son of doting parents and taught to believe in himself, he'd taken their lectures to heart. Maybe too much.

To hear him tell it, Anson could do no wrong. The fact that he followed words with actions only made dealing with him that much worse. Dex tolerated his cousin's attitude because he loved the guy, and he had to admit Anson was a lot of fun.

Jack suggested Anson do something anatomically impossible to himself, to which Anson responded with an obscene gesture.

"You guys are a riot." Dex drained his beer and ordered another. With his height and weight, it took nearly a six pack to get him close to buzzed. But he didn't want to get drunk, just mellow out and relax with the guys…while getting some much-needed intel. "Jack, tell me about Maya."

"Here we go." Anson motioned for another round of drinks. "Barely back in town and he's at it again."

"Please. Like I'm the only one. Don't even pretend it's nothing but chance you're building a restaurant next to sexy Riley Hewitt."

Dex had always liked Ann and Riley. Ann, a petite redhead with eyes for his best bud, and Riley, the dark-skinned beauty he alternated naughty dreams with Maya about. As he'd matured, he still considered Riley beautiful. The woman could cook anyone under the table and from what he'd heard worked harder than anyone he'd known to finance her own bakery. Even in high school she'd known what she wanted to do.

Dex on the other hand had known *who* he wanted to do. He grinned at the bad pun. Photography had been his first love, next to Maya. Now that he had the one, he intended to snag and keep the other.

Jack looked from him to Anson, his brow raised. "So you want info on Maya or Riley? Or both?" he asked with a smirk aimed at Anson.

Anson glared back. "I need to take a piss." He hopped from his seat and disappeared.

"Anger issues." Jack shook his head.

"Impatient bastard." Dex laughed. "But he's family. Now tell me about Maya."

"Impatient bastard," Jack repeated with a grin. "She's still snarky, unattached and sexy as hell. You sure you know what you're in for trying to land her?"

"Do I question your attraction to a woman I'd fear squashing in bed? I mean, dude, she's so little."

Jack's smile widened. "Just perfect for me. But I take your point. Maya… Hmm. You know she's only got her dad."

"Right. Her mom died when she was a kid." But he didn't know much more than that. Her mother had to have been Native American, because her dad was Caucasian. Not a bad-looking guy, but Maya had clearly inherited most of her features from her mother.

"Yeah. You know her dad, of course. Great guy. He's friends with my parents and Riley's mom. Probably a support group to get through the Terrible Trio's growing years." They both laughed. "Those girls are still thick as thieves. You take one, you kind of inherit the others. But I love that about Ann. She's loyal and has terrific friends."

"Just like you," Dex pointed out.

"Oh yeah. My friends are great."

They both looked up as a growling Anson sat back down. Anson flagged down a server and barked an order for another beer, which arrived in seconds from a nervous waiter.

Dex turned back to Jack. "So Maya. No steady guys?"

Anson kept his mouth shut, thankfully, and nursed a second beer while Jack filled him in.

"They don't last long. Woman is rough on men. She's nice enough, but I get the feeling she gets bored easily. Try not to be so nice, Dex. That might help."

Dex frowned. "I'm not nice."

Anson choked on his beer. "You're kidding, right? Did you or did you not help an old lady across the street yesterday?"

He flushed. "She'd lost her cane. Gimme a break."

Jack coughed but didn't quite hide his laughter. "Polite is good. Boring is bad. Maya likes 'em a bit rough."

"I was in the Corps." He knew how to handle himself just fine.

"And you can be a bit of an asshole. You're in," Anson said drily. "In fact, now that I think about it, you and Maya are perfect for each other."

"You know, you'd be a lot more convincing as a dickhead if you weren't being so helpful with my studio."

"Whatever."

Jack poked him. "Tell me more about the new place. How's it going?"

"You know I'm getting into portraits."

"Mundane photography," Anson murmured. "The man's lost his edge."

"Not mundane. Local stuff. Weddings, portraits, stuff like that. My downtown location is perfect for walk-ins or appointments. At first it'll just be me, but I plan to hire on some help."

"Nice." Jack gave him a thumbs-up. "I know you won a bunch of awards from those overseas shots in Afghanistan."

Dex shrugged. "Feels like a lifetime ago. Don't get me wrong. I still plan to do the heavier stuff. Some wildlife and nature photos when I make trips to Asia and Africa. But mostly I want to settle down here."

"Near *Ma-ya*," Anson added in a singsong voice.

Dex just looked at him. "I know you don't want to go there."

Anson shook his head but shut up and watched the hockey game on the TV overhead.

When Jack frowned in question, Dex mouthed *Riley*.

Jack nodded. "Right. So what else can I tell you about Maya? Hmm. Let me think. She's still competitive. Still addicted to coffee. Has a soft spot for dogs and kids, go figure. At Halloween she gave out too much candy and Ann kept bitching at her to slow down. But of course they ran out, because our neighborhood is crazy at the holidays."

"I thought about buying in there, but it would have to be the right place."

"For the right girl." Anson sighed. "Are you sure you're set on her? I know a shitload of women who would love you. You have your own job, your own car, money, don't live with your parents and aren't paying four different child support payments a month. The *coup de grace*, you're related to me. You could be rolling in pussy if you wanted."

"Now isn't that an image." Dex grimaced. "Thank you, but I can get my own dates. I'm not interested in easy or expensive."

"Hooker is not a four letter word," Anson said.

"Neither is girlfriend, you moron."

Jack laughed at them. "Oh man. I used to be you two. Wanting what I can't have. Then I nabbed her."

"Lucky prick." Dex wished he could be as happy as Jack. But he had a plan—to keep Maya on her toes by continuing to force her to date him.

"Exactly how did that blackmail happen again?" Jack asked. "I was with Ann in the back room in your studio when it went down. Something about Selena's face?"

"It was a thing of beauty," Anson admitted.

Dex frowned. "I thought you said you didn't see anything."

"I saw everything. Selena was mouthing off, then Maya belted her in the face. Broke her nose with a classic punch."

None of them had liked Selena, and they liked her even less now since she'd just divorced—and raked over the coals—a friend of theirs.

"Yeah, well, before Maya could tackle her to the ground, I grabbed her and stopped her from making things worse. Anson backed me up. We said Selena walked into a door."

"Her lawsuits are over, by the way. She knows she can't win."

"Good." Dex met Anson's raised glass with his own. "Now with Selena out of the way, I can focus on seducing Maya. I finally got that kiss I was denied at prom." *And it was everything I'd hoped for.* "That's right, gentlemen." He ignored Anson's groan. "I'm calling dibs. Maya is mine."

Jack had already staked his claim on Ann. "Guess that just leaves Riley for Anson. Oh wait. She hates your guts. Sucks to be you."

"She doesn't hate me."

Dex refused to cut his cousin any slack. "She sure doesn't like you. Face it. You screwed up. Instead of trying to be nice and just talking with the woman, you kept trying to outdo her at every turn."

"I was trying to impress her," Anson admitted. "But that was a long time ago. I grew out of the need back when I was a teenager."

"Uh-huh. Not believing you."

Jack shook his head. "Me neither. Come on, Anson. Try to be a little nicer around her. Just think. The three of them are friends. The three of us are friends. Ann's already bringing up date nights with other couples. I want to hang myself at the thought of doubling with her principal and her husband. The woman is forty going on ninety. God save me from cat people. But you guys? Hook up with Maya and Riley and I won't have to shoot myself when we're 'Camping with Couples'." He ended in air quotes. "Just think. No annoying Harvard types or rabid athletes trying to show us up. Well, that's if Anson can tone down his need to be better than the rest of the world."

"Up yours, Jack."

"He's got you there," Dex admitted.

"I'm not trying. I *am* better than everyone else."

"Except Riley," Dex added.

This time, Anson didn't argue with him. He just grunted and drank.

"Right. So, Jack, I have nine more dates with Maya to get her to love me forever. You're in with the best friend. Any suggestions?"

"Besides an exorcism?" Anson quipped under his breath, which Jack found hilarious.

Dex tried to look stern, but he couldn't stop a smile. "Come on. She's not that bad."

"Cuz, at least be honest. She's a holy terror. She *broke a woman's nose*," Anson emphasized.

"So she has a few anger issues," Dex defended. "Who doesn't?"

"Well, when Ann gets mad, she freezes me out." Jack shrugged. "And I've seen Riley refuse to bake cookies when she's upset with someone. Not exactly the violent types."

"Maybe so. But no one, and I mean no one, has ever kissed me the way Maya did Friday night. That woman wants me. I want her. How hard can grabbing hold of her be?"

"Catching a tiger by the tail," Anson sighed.

Jack nodded. "It's not the grabbing, it's the holding on for dear life you should be worried about."

Dex said nothing, still feeling enthusiastic about the prospect.

Jack and Anson stared at him before Jack called for another round.

Anson shook his head, then he and Jack raised their near-empty glasses to Dex in a toast. "For my naïve sap of a cousin. May you survive this battle."

"Against all odds," Jack continued. "May you not find yourself castrated, crying and broken when she's through with you."

"Poor bastard."

A waiter brought them another round of beers. But while Jack and Anson continued to tease him, Dex planned to outflank and out-strategize his opponent. Mean she might be, but Dex had staying power. And by damn, he was a Marine.

What more needed to be said?

Chapter Four

Monday morning Dex puttered around his new studio, eager to open for business. He planned to officially open his doors in another week, though he'd already gotten a few early appointments for Christmas cards and two weddings.

The domestic nature of his photography was such a change from the dynamic and sometimes dangerous shots of urban life and nature he'd taken overseas. Africa, Asia, Russia, Europe, he'd traveled extensively while in the Corps and then while out of it, capturing life as he saw it.

Photography had always been his passion. Despite his time in the service, he'd continued to shoot pictures whenever possible. And the work had paid off. Literally. He'd managed to grab the attention of a big-name agent who'd sold his work in galleries worldwide.

Yet something had always been missing. He loved to travel. He loved his art. But he'd never felt at home like he did in Bend, near his family. Near Maya.

He sighed. The woman would flip out if he admitted he'd returned for her. In love with her as a kid but unaware of the true depth of his feelings, it had taken time for him to realize he wanted Maya in his life.

Despite the distance between them, he'd kept subtle tabs on her via his mother. He'd worried she might find someone, but she hadn't. He thought he knew why. The woman had some serious hang-ups, not just about relationships, but about her identity as well.

Someone knocked on the outer door of the studio, interrupting his train of thought.

As if he'd summoned her, Maya stood outside holding two cups of coffee.

He smiled, his grin widening as her frown grew. He hurried to unlock and open the door, then ushered her inside. "Good morning, beautiful."

"Here." She shoved a cup at him.

"Still not a morning person, I take it?"

She shook her head.

He took a sip of his coffee and nearly spit it out.

"Oh, that's probably mine. You drink yours black, right?" She switched cups and he drank the dark stuff with pleasure.

"Perfect. Thanks."

She shrugged, a casual gesture that sent her black hair over her shoulder like a ripple of silk. "I came downtown to talk to my accountant. Thought I'd swing by and see what you're up to."

He had the space divided up. In the front was a small area for a reception desk and waiting area complete with a couch, chairs and a table. In the back, several sections had been divided by expanses of wall, where he snapped portraits, and behind that, a storage room for supplies.

She walked into the back. After locking the front door, he followed her. She trailed a hand over a few set pieces, and he once again experienced an overwhelming urge to toss her against the nearest wall and take her. She wore a long skirt over brown boots and a sweater that looked soft to the touch. Her breasts, large, round, and so appealing, fit her frame perfectly. Maya constantly tempted him to touch, indulge and not come up for air until he turned sixty. At least.

He coughed to clear his throat and prayed his jeans masked his arousal. "Thanks for the coffee."

"Sure." She stopped by the back corner, where he'd hung a few prints taken during his stint in Germany. Ancient castles in full fields of green surrounded by clear sky. Like a fairy tale come to life. "I like this one."

"Pretty grand, eh? I liked the structure of it, the hard lines softened by the flora behind it."

She smiled. "Well don't you sound all artistic?"

He took a sip of his coffee to keep himself from reaching for her. "Something we have in common then."

"Yeah, but my stuff is pretty basic."

"I wouldn't call your work basic."

"It's just clay."

"If it's so basic, why isn't everyone as successful as you are?" He knew Maya made a living off her art, and by any creative person's standards that counted as success. The term *starving artist* hadn't been coined by accident.

She flushed and turned away. If he hadn't been looking closely, he would have missed her reaction. The woman responded to praise like a child staring longingly through a toyshop window, wanting something out of reach. It saddened and angered him that she never accepted her due, rather she shrugged compliments away as if she didn't deserve them. That hadn't changed in the time he'd been away either.

"I'm not rolling in riches like you. I'm living okay, I guess." She moved away from him toward another print in the corner, a vibrant picture of the setting sun over the Cathedral of Basil the Blessed in Moscow. "Did you really go there?"

"Yeah. Gorgeous detail. Russia's a beautiful place." He

moved closer to her and didn't stop until he stood directly behind her. "It's full of warmth, but most people only think of its cold and unforgiving climate. It's not all Siberia in the middle of winter."

She stiffened, no doubt feeling him right behind her, then turned around and put a hand on his chest. "Whoa. A little close, aren't you, Black?"

"Not close enough." He leaned in slowly, to give her time to move away should she want space. He planned to seduce her at a leisurely pace. From her reaction to their kiss in the truck, he thought he'd been making headway. Great on the one hand, yet doing no more than kissing her left him aching.

It was too tempting to have her so close. He set his coffee down on the nearby table, then took hers and put it down as well. Eliminating the small distance between them, he gave in to desire and kissed her.

She let him, let the heat build between them, then gripped his shoulders and pushed him back.

He didn't release her, not sure at what point his hands had gripped her by the waist. "Now isn't that better than a cup of coffee?" He tried to joke off his desire, but the glare she shot him told him he'd overstepped.

"No."

Damn it. Before he could apologize, she yanked him forward and kissed *him*. She took charge, penetrating his mouth, licking and stroking until he felt himself taken, seduced and thoroughly overwhelmed. *Jesus Christ.*

She pulled back, her eyes so dark they looked black. "*That's* better than a cup of coffee."

"I'll do you one better," he growled and shoved her back against the wall. He plastered his mouth to hers, determined to be the one in charge. Maya as the aggressor sent his body into overdrive…and recharged his kink to dominate.

Knowing how strong she was, wondering how much

she could truly take, made his need to control her an all-encompassing urge.

Then her hands snaked under his sweater. She scraped her nails up his chest, plucked at his nipples, then trailed down his belly, sliding past his jeans and underwear to graze his cockhead.

He hissed his approval, and she dug deeper, trying to touch more of him. He hadn't planned to have sex with her until at least date five, but damn if his cock remembered that. He couldn't deny needs long buried. He fucking wanted her with every breath he had. With every cell in his body.

He trailed his lips to her ear and whispered, "If you don't want to be fucked up against this wall right now, you need to pull your hands away and leave."

She responded by finding his cock and gripping him tight.

He shuddered, closed his eyes, then nipped her earlobe. "That's all the warning you're gonna get." Pulling back, he studied her, noting her full lips, the shine of desire in her eyes, her heavy breathing... "Take off your top. Let me see those tits."

His vulgarity excited her, as he'd guessed it would. She bit her lower lip and immediately took off her top. The sight of her full breasts made him want to worship them for days. He didn't wait for her to get to her bra but unfastened it himself. Then he stared.

She didn't flinch or shy away. Proud Maya stood as if she'd been meant to be admired this way.

"Shit." Not the most articulate thing to say, but seeing those beautiful breasts, her dark nipples tight and drawn in arousal, took away his ability to think. He lowered his head and took a nipple in his mouth while frantically praying he had a condom in his wallet.

Her moans and pleas for more undid him. He continued to suck her nipple while pushing her skirt down her body. She kicked it off, and he pulled back to see her dressed in high brown boots and a fucking thong.

"Jesus. Am I dreaming?" He didn't wait for her answer. Instead he knelt, dragged her thong off and drew her sweet clit into his mouth.

She clutched his head while he ate her out. He continued to taste her while he shoved one finger, then two inside her, loving her impossibly tight pussy. When she cried out and came, he eagerly lapped her up.

Unable to wait any longer, he fished a condom out of his wallet—thank God—and donned it in seconds.

"Damn, Dex." She reached out to him, and he went more than willingly. He pushed her back against the wall and kissed her, knowing she tasted herself on his lips. So damn hot.

He lifted her easily, aware the only things she wore were the pair of boots she crossed behind his back. Then he angled himself at her wet core and shoved hard.

"Fuck me. You feel so good," he groaned as he took her.

She didn't answer, moaning as she gripped him tighter, riding him as much as he pounded into her.

He kissed his way to her breasts again, sucking her nipples while an explosive orgasm built up, creeping along his spine.

"Dex, yes. Yes," she cried.

He released her nipple and clutched her ass tighter, trying to get as deep inside her as he could. "Coming, baby," he warned as he shoved one more time and climaxed.

He saw stars as he pumped into her, wishing he'd been coming naked into her wet warmth. Yet even separated by a thin bit of latex, he felt her heat. The orgasm so intense his knees nearly buckled.

When he could breathe again, he leaned against her, refusing to pull out just yet.

"Wow, Dex. I didn't know you had that in you."

He ignored making an immature refrain about having it

in *her* and just nodded. He felt her fingers thread through his hair and moaned at the pleasure of having her all to himself. He'd made love to Maya Werner. Against a wall in his studio. A less romantic place he couldn't fathom, and it had been beyond his fantasies.

"Dex? Are you still hard?" She blinked at him, then smiled. "Well, well. I do love a man with endurance."

He tried not to think too much and just revel in Maya. "I wasn't expecting this. I only had the one condom."

"And you're wearing it. Too bad." She gave him a fake pout.

"But there are other things we can do." He gave her a sly smile. "Unless you're only good for one round?"

"Please. I have yet to meet a man who can keep up with me."

"Challenge on, baby." He withdrew from her and took off the condom. He dropped it to the floor and stroked himself, excited when she continued to watch him jerking off. "Go on. Touch yourself. Let's see who comes first."

She looked away from his cock to stare at him. Then her smile turned carnal. Dark. "You think I won't?"

"I pray you will."

"Well, I propose something else."

"Yeah?" He'd grown hard too easily. Touching himself in front of Maya was keeping him that way, as if his first explosive orgasm hadn't happened.

"How about I jerk you off, and you finger me? Then we'll see who comes first."

Hell yeah. "Wager?"

"I'd say whoever comes first is already the winner."

He grinned. "You got that right." With pleasure, he reached for her wet folds and slid his large fingers between them. She widened her stance to give him better access, and then she reached for his cock and pumped him. Long, slow strokes that drove him mad.

Rubbing her clit faster as his excitement increased, he stared into her eyes, still not sure he was awake as his dream come true continued to progress.

"You're drenching my fingers," he whispered. "So wet and hot. Wait 'til I come inside that hot pussy. My big cock wearing you out."

She squirmed, her breath raspy, but she didn't break eye contact.

"I'm wet for you. My mouth is wet too, Dex. Imagine how good it'll feel when I'm licking you. Sucking that fat cock until you come down my throat. Yeah, you like that, don't you?"

He'd never been so hard. Then the witch jerked him faster, and he couldn't slow down. Couldn't stop himself from crying her name as he jerked and came all over her belly and hand.

He kissed her as he continued to spend and shoved his middle finger inside her while he ground his thumb against her clit. When he pulled his mouth away, she finally let his cock go and humped his hand.

"Fuck. Oh yeah, I'm coming," she said on a gasp. She trembled against him, her clit hard and full, her body wet with need. He'd helped her to her own happy ending again, and her pleasure made his that much better.

"You okay?" he asked after pulling his fingers away.

"Hold on," she said and closed her eyes. "Still not thinking straight."

He chuckled and kissed her, a soft kiss of thanks. He studied her, still amazed at the way his morning had started, especially since none of this had been planned.

"You are fucking beautiful." He slid a hand over her belly, rubbing his seed over her skin. A primitive thrill of possession filled him—the need to claim her, to let everyone know Maya Werner belonged to him—and was difficult to ignore. But handling her the right way now would set the tone for how they moved on.

He knew how her mind worked. If he let Maya control the relationship, she'd find some way to reject him and move on, not giving them a chance.

"So, Dex, I—"

"Our date tomorrow night. I'm thinking pizza. That work for you?"

She frowned. "You still want those dates?"

"Why wouldn't I?"

"Well, we just…"

"Fucked? Yeah, we did. And we'll do it again."

She raised a brow in a way that always made him want to tie her up and punish her for her arrogance. And now that he knew what it felt like to have her, he wanted nothing more than to share his fantasies with her.

"Sex between us should be my call, not yours," she said in a tone that went with her raised brow.

"How so?" He tucked his cock back in his pants, amazed at how much he'd come, and felt ready for a nap. Stifling a grin, he straightened the rest of his clothing, loving the fact she still had nothing on but her heeled boots.

"Well, you call the shots on our 'dates'. Seems to me this qualifies as a date, and you specifically said no sex on our dates. So I should manage our time together, to make sure you don't take advantage of me again." Before he could take offense, she grinned at him. "I mean, all that body and that huge cock, what's a horny girl going to do but jump your bones?"

He smiled with her. "Tell you what. You can pick the location of our next dinner date. I promise not to have sex with you or wear tight and revealing clothing. Then you won't be tempted to jump me again."

"Where's the fun in that?"

This Maya delighted him. Fun, flirty, and she seemed to have let down her guard for once. Perhaps he'd do best to make love to her at every opportunity. A win-win.

He grinned.

She slowly put her clothing on, making no effort to wipe him off her skin. "Okay, we'll meet at Polvino's Pizza on the westside."

He frowned. "That's not a restaurant. That's a pizza place. They do takeout."

"Yes, and there's an outdoor food court across the street. We can eat great pizza by a fire pit before walking back to my place."

"Your place?" He gave a mock frown. "But what if you're tempted to do bad things to me?" He stretched out, pleased when she followed his movements with her gaze. "I'm just a man. If you try to trick me into sex with you again, I'll probably fall for it."

She smiled. "Sounds good to me."

"Fine." He sighed. "If I have to."

"Oh come on."

"Six o'clock, Polvino's. I'm buying."

"Obviously." She flipped her hair over her shoulder and left him watching her.

The door closed, and she was gone.

He stared at the walls, looking at the pictures but not seeing them. *I just fucked Maya. Twice. And she was beyond amazing.* He grinned. Then he started to laugh.

After the joy settled to a pleasurable hum throughout his body, he realized he needed to rethink his strategy with the sexy woman. If left to Maya, she'd fuck him until he couldn't think. He'd end up telling her how much she meant to him. Then she'd drop his ass cold and move on—no commitment, no vulnerability.

He'd have to make sure to keep her on her toes. Much

as it pained him to do it, he'd have to refrain from having sex with her tomorrow night.

He picked up the condom off the floor and tossed it in the trash. No more sex with Maya? Dear God, could he do it—er, not do it? Maybe to be on the safe side, he'd get more protection.

A jumbo pack this time.

Chapter Five

Tuesday night his cousin continued to harass him all the way to Polvino's pizzeria. "Classy date you're going on, Dex." Anson snorted. "You going to splurge and let her have pepperoni too?"

"Shut up. At least my date will talk to me. Your lady love dreams about staking you in your sleep."

Anson frowned. "She does not."

"Yeah, that's harsh. More like a bullet to the brain. I can't see Riley getting all up and in your face. She's too nice for that."

"First of all, she's not my lady love."

Who did Anson think he was kidding? He'd had the hots for Riley forever.

"And second," Anson continued, "Riley is a mutual acquaintance, nothing more. We're business neighbors."

"Business neighbors? Dude, you had an entire city to plant a new restaurant. Why move right next to Riley? I'll tell you why," Dex said before his cousin could comment. "Because you're finally sacking up. You want her, and you can't stand that she doesn't want you. So this is your subtle way of making your move. Only you're a complete moron and it's backfiring on you."

"You can deflect all you want, but tonight has nothing to do with Riley."

"Never said it did." Dex grinned, always in a good mood when he could peeve his cousin. Anson was a terrific person and one of his best friends, but he was also his own worst enemy. The guy didn't know how to be anything but the best at whatever he did. Money, work, women, Anson had it all, and he knew it. But Riley had never given him the time of day, and poor Anson had no idea how to handle that.

"Why am I doing you this favor again?" Anson asked as he turned onto Galveston.

"Because I didn't want to drive, my love life needs help and you're Mr. Fix It."

"I thought I was a complete moron."

"That too."

"Oh, right." Anson grinned. "So your scheme—"

"Plan."

"*Tawdry* scheme is to continue blackmailing Maya into what? Falling in love with you?"

"Yep."

"That makes no sense."

"Sure it does. Maya hasn't changed all that much since high school. She's still beautiful, guarded and in control of every aspect of her life. In a lot of ways, you and she are alike."

"Oh?"

"Yeah. You're both too cocky for your own good."

"Please. Just because I'm self-confident and feel no need to brush off my many accomplishments, people—"

"There it is. That boasting, not that it isn't well-deserved."

"Thanks for that at least," Anson said with no small amount of sarcasm. "I still don't see why you don't have a rational conversation with the woman. Just tell her how you feel. You're smart, have the family looks and a big wallet. What's not to like?"

Dex shook his head. "You dumb bastard. You have met Maya, right? She has a thing about control. Luckily for her, I do too. And I don't mind letting her think she has it."

Anson glanced at him then pulled into a parking spot. "Good luck. With that one, you're going to need it. You sure you wouldn't rather have someone else? I know a lot of people. Carla's a great girl. Debbie too. Both independent, cute and pleasant."

"Pleasant is boring. I like 'em a little mean." He looked through the windshield and saw Maya waiting out front, tapping her foot. "This one's mine."

"My poor cousin. She's going to chew you up and spit you out."

"But she'll have her mouth on some part of me, so it's all good."

Anson chuckled. "Dumbass. You have your own ride home then?"

"From Maya's it's maybe a ten minute walk. I'll be fine." He opened the door.

"Famous last words." Anson shoved him out. "Talk to you later...if you're still breathing that is." He nodded at Maya, who nodded back.

She glared at Dex. "You're late."

"And hello to you too." Dex smiled, oddly pleased when she frowned back at him. She looked cautious, and he couldn't have been happier. Their time in his shop had meant more than a measly fuck to her if Maya wasn't sure how to handle him.

"I want pizza." She glanced in the window at a kid flipping dough.

"After you." Dex held the door for her, amused when she

strutted past him with her nose in the air. Then her perfume hit him and he had to contain a groan. She smelled so damn good.

He ordered with her, and they took their pizza across the street into the open food court. Tables and chairs littered the central space, while around the court several food trucks served patrons daily until ten at night. "You want a beer?"

"Is snow white?"

He smiled. "Any preference?"

"Whatever you're having. I'm not picky." She gave him a look that said she included him in that comment.

He laughed and left, returning with two drafts. "Here, Ms. Picky."

She smirked and took the cup he handed her. "Thanks."

They ate together in quiet, watching the people around them. A few families with small children. Couples, a group of men arguing over football and a bunch of teenagers enjoying the crisp fall air. A huge fire blazed in the very center of the yard, while a few propane heaters around the outlying tables provided heat.

"I like this."

She glanced at him and nodded. "Me too. It's *tres* casual." She smiled. "I bet you're wishing you had your camera with you."

He blinked. "How did you know?"

"You have that look."

"What look?"

She finished a slice of pizza before answering. "That look, the one that's always studying everyone. Looking for angles or lighting or whatever it is you see through a lens."

He liked the fact she knew his expressions enough to peg him, because yeah, he'd been thinking what a great black and white shot this setting would have made. But as he stared at her, he thought how amazing she'd look silhouetted against the moon.

"Dex?" She took a healthy swig of beer. "You still with me or are you zoning out again?"

"Now how could I zone out when I'm sitting with the prettiest girl in Bend?"

She rolled her eyes. "Does that line ever work on anyone?"

"First time using it. What do you think?"

"Don't quit your day job."

He laughed. "I won't, trust me. I had such a great day yesterday." She choked on her beer. "Thought I wouldn't mention it, huh?"

She shrugged. "Not like what we did is a big secret or anything." She paused. "What did Anson think?"

"I don't kiss and tell." He held a hand over his heart, pretending she'd broken it. "How dare you think I would?"

She laughed. "Save it, Dex. We both know you're proud of how you wrecked me the other day."

"I did, didn't I?" His grin widened. "What did Riley and Ann think of my performance?"

She frowned. "We're not a bunch of magpies, you know. We don't share everything." He raised a brow and she snapped, "We don't."

"Look, I don't mind." He put a touch of hurt into his next words. "I'm not ashamed of what we did."

"I'm not either. But I… You're screwing with me, aren't you?"

"Isn't it obvious?" He laughed at her and drank his beer. "You're so fun to tease."

Her cheeks darkened. "Shut up and eat your pizza."

He razzed her some more as they ate, but when he started to ask about her day, she looked past him, mouth agape. He turned to look behind him.

"Dad?" Maya said. "What are you doing here?"

Roy Werner stood with a petite blonde on his arm.

"Hello, honey. And who's this?" His eyes narrowed. "Dexter Black? Wow, did you get big. I heard you were back in town."

"Hey, Mr. Werner. Great to see you again." Dex stood and shook Roy's hand.

"Roy, please. Oh, and this is Bev. Bev, meet Dexter and my daughter, Maya. We decided to take in the great weather and the food."

"Hello." Bev smiled. "Nice to meet you both."

Dex greeted her warmly, but Maya seemed a little standoffish, though neither her father nor Bev seemed to notice.

"We don't want to bother—" her father started to say.

"Why don't you join us?" Maya invited.

"I'm fine with that," said Bev, "unless we're interrupting?"

Dex glanced at Maya, who smirked at him. "No, that's fine. Please join us. Your company is more than welcome."

Bev, at least, wasn't immune to his charm. She sat while Roy went to get them something to eat. "So, Maya, your father has been telling me that you're an artist?"

Maya took a long sip of beer, watching Bev.

Dex watched the scene play out, wondering if the stubborn woman would be intentionally rude or if she'd play nice. Apparently she didn't mean to play nice with *him*, inviting others into their private time.

"I'm an artist, yeah." Maya nodded. "I work with clay, primarily. But sometimes I delve into other mediums."

"Oh? That's really interesting."

"Not as interesting as Poindexter here." She thrust a thumb in Dex's direction.

"Poindexter? Really?" He hated that stupid nickname.

Maya grinned. "Dex is a famous photographer."

"Don't deflect, Maya." He turned to Bev. "Maya's been in art shows all over the Northwest, and she's had pieces in a ton of galleries. The big ones in Tumalo and Sisters, Fobragios in

Portland, and a few in Seattle, right, Maya?"

She stared at him. "How do you know all that?"

"I know things." Dex gave her a smug smile.

"Really? Well did you know I'm still hungry?" She snatched his third piece of pizza off his plate.

"Predator," he mumbled, and she laughed at him as she ate his piece.

Bev chuckled. "How long have you two been dating?"

"A billion years," Maya said at the same time Dex answered, "Not long enough."

Again, Bev laughed.

"What about you and my dad? You two already shacked up or what?" Maya asked.

The silence that settled over the table felt heavy, until Bev grinned. "You don't hold back, do you? Roy warned me that I'd like you."

Dex let out a quiet sigh of relief. Good thing Roy had chosen a woman with thick skin.

"Your father handled some business for my late husband years ago, and when I found myself needing financial advice, he was the guy I knew would shoot straight with me. Then, well, you of all people know how charming he can be."

Roy returned with a tray of Thai food and drinks. He set Bev up before helping himself to dinner. "What did I miss?"

Roy had height, probably where Maya had gotten hers, as well as an olive complexion, light brown eyes and dark brown hair. A handsome-enough guy who looked far younger than what had to be his late fifties or early sixties. He was a financial planner for one of the big names and a whiz when it came to money. Dex had always liked him because the man didn't tolerate nonsense—especially not from his obstinate daughter.

"Maya was asking Bev how long you two have shacked up," Dex said helpfully.

"Maya, really?" Her father shook his head.

She glared at Dex before turning a sweet smile on her father. "Well, you never saw fit to mention her, so I thought I'd go for her intentions right away. Don't want anyone taking advantage of my poor daddy."

Dex choked on his beer. Boy was she laying it on thick. A little bratty for a woman her age. Her attitude made him want to take her back home and spank the hell out of her ass before sliding inside her. He shifted in his seat.

Roy just looked at her. "For your information, Bev is very comfortable, with or without me. She should be careful around *me*, because we all know how money-hungry I am."

Maya suddenly looked bored. "Oh." Then she looked at Bev. "He's all yours."

Bev chuckled. "You sound just like my oldest boy. He's always staring down any man I go to dinner with, giving him 'The Talk'."

"It usually works. I can be very unpleasant," Maya told her.

"She can," Dex agreed. "Witness."

Roy laughed. "I always liked you, Dexter. Dexter took Maya to the prom her senior year," he told Bev. "They made such a cute couple."

"Beauty and the geek," Dex said with self-deprecating humor. "I was a lot smaller then."

"But just as geeky," Maya added with a grin.

Roy dug into his food. "So what have you been up to? How long are you in town?"

Before Dex could answer, Maya did for him. "He's back to stay. Apparently genius boy is setting up a photography studio downtown, on Bond."

"That's great." Bev beamed at him.

"Yeah, and he's loaded." Maya nudged her head in Dex's direction. "So, Bev, you can do a lot better than my dad. Just sayin'."

"Maya." Roy frowned.

Dex couldn't help laughing. "But, Maya, you're so charming and demure. I don't want anyone but you, sugar plum."

Roy and Bev seemed to get a kick out of that. Maya didn't seem as amused, then he caught sight of the smile she tried to hide. "Yep. She's the most disagreeable, pain-in-the-butt, temperamental artist I've ever met. And a more gifted craftsman I've never seen."

Maya flushed.

"She's not bad on the eyes either," he added and watched her blush deepen.

"Ha. He's got you pegged." Roy pointed a finger at her. "Looks like her mother. Same attitude and everything. But she has my work ethic, so it all evens out."

At mention of Maya's mother, her expression turned flat.

"She must have been beautiful," Bev said.

"She was." Maya smiled, but he could tell it was forced.

Roy nodded. "I told you she passed away a few years after Maya was born. Then I was stuck handling this bundle of energy."

Dex wanted to laugh at the description. Bundle of energy? He'd always pictured Maya as more like a cat. Sensual, slinky and devious. From what he'd nagged out of Riley, the girl liked her beauty sleep and had no problem doing nothing all day long. But once an artistic frenzy hit, watch out. She'd pounce on her work and not let up until she nailed it.

Her father and Bev turned the conversation toward how they'd met, and Maya relaxed a little. But Dex wondered about the tension he'd witnessed.

After a while, he and Maya left her father and Bev with a promise for dinner in a few weeks. As they left the food court, he reached for Maya's hand and gripped it tight, expecting her to try and pull away.

"Hey, I let you invite them to water down our date. You owe me," he said.

"Water down?"

"You're a slick one, I'll give you that. So where are we headed next? A walk to Newport?" He liked how her hand felt under his. Smaller, slighter, yet strong. Maya had little give to her, and he couldn't wait to test her boundaries.

"My place." She gripped his hand harder, stroking her thumb along his knuckle.

Sad how her simple touch made him so hard. If he lost his wits for even a second, she'd have him on his knees and begging.

"Your place for some conversation, right?" He glanced down at her. "Remember, you're the one who said no sex while we're dating."

"I did say that, didn't I? But plans can change." She winked at him, and he suddenly found it uncomfortable to walk in his too-tight jeans.

"Let's talk about something I find fascinating."

"Besides me?"

"Indirectly. Tell me about your mom."

That teasing sense of fun left her face. "Why?"

"Because I want to know more about you. This is a date where we talk. Have fun. No sex."

She frowned. "Sex is fun. My mother is not fun. She's dead."

"Right. And she died…what? Twenty-some years ago? Tell me about her."

"Nothing to tell." She tried to tug her hand from his and scowled when he refused to let go. "She had me. She left. She died. Happy now?"

She left? "How did she die?" he asked.

"Car accident. I barely remember her. It's just been dad

and me for years. I doubt Bev will last longer than six or seven months. That's his M.O."

"Yeah? What's yours?"

She squeezed his hand. "If I'm not bored out of my mind by date two, I try on the guy for size. If he's not bad at sex, I can usually go a few months before losing my patience. Then we split."

"And you're happy with that?"

"Don't judge. What about you?"

"I'm not judging. I'm asking a question."

She shrugged. "I'm not upset about it. It is what it is. I'm not a long-term-relationship girl. If that's what you're angling for, go somewhere else."

"Now why would I do that when I have the sexy Maya Werner by my side?"

She blew out a loud breath. "You're cute but annoying."

"So it will say on my tombstone one day."

She chuckled.

"Anyway, to answer your question in a non-defensive manner—unlike some people—I've had a few long-standing relationships. But my career came first for me when I was in the service. Then my trips abroad made it difficult to be in a steady relationship."

"But now you're home. Looking for a wife and two-point-five kids?"

"You forgot the white picket fence."

She snorted. "Figures."

"As usual, you made a wrong assumption. I'm not looking for a wife, kids and home. I'm setting up for a new phase in my life. I'm back with family and friends, have a steady job, and eventually I'll find Mrs. Black."

"No rush?"

He glanced down at her, intrigued by her deliberate casual air. "No rush." *Not when I'm already holding her hand.*

"That's good." She cleared her throat, her hand feeling warm in his. "I mean, it's like people turn thirty and feel the need to race to the altar. Hell. I don't ever plan to get married. I'm good with how things are now."

"And how are they?"

She shot him a sly glance. "I get sex whenever I want. I don't answer to anybody and do what I want. I'm still in my 'all about me' years."

"Which implies someday you'll be out of those years."

"Yeah, then I'll be into my traveling phase. So again, no ties to any one guy. I'm too free-thinking for that anyway."

"Oh? So you're an orgy girl?"

She punched him in the arm. "No, jackass. I just don't need a man by my side to be happy."

"Never thought you needed one to be happy, but it's nice to have someone special to share things with, isn't it?"

She shrugged. "I guess. Why all the heavy chatter?"

"Just making small talk. Why so defensive?"

"I'm not defensive." He just looked at her until she swore. "Fuck off. I'm not."

"Uh-huh." They walked in silence, nearing her home. "So why are we heading to your house, exactly?"

She smiled at him, and he felt like a mouse being hunted by a large, hungry cat. "To talk. You're all about communicating, aren't you? That's what these dates are about. Us getting to know each other, right?"

"Yes." *I know what you're up to, Maya. But it won't work.* She stroked his hand again, and he contained a shiver.

"Nope. Not gonna happen."

"What?" she asked, all innocence.

"Nothing. Now where were we?"

"We're here," she said as they approached an aging Craftsman-style house on the edge of a cul-de-sac. "Welcome to my home."

"Said the spider to the fly," he muttered.

She grinned and unlocked the door, then pushed it open and stood back, waiting for him to go in first. "Don't be scared, baby. I promise not to hurt you. Much."

He frowned at her as he entered, ignoring her laugh. *I won't touch her. I won't. I can't. Must. Stay. Strong.*

He had to convince himself to remain firm, hearing the soft snick of her door closing and the overloud sound of the lock sealing them together. Alone. In private.

This was going to be a long night.

Chapter Six

Now that she had him all to herself, she didn't know where to start. She hadn't been able to stop thinking about him since yesterday, when he'd made her see stars.

If only she could have kept her prurient curiosity to his body. Picture him just as a walking pleasure machine. All brawn, no brain. But she kept wondering what he did in his spare time, what he liked to eat and drink, his favorite sports, how his parents had fared in his absence, if he thought about her...

She forced herself to stop thinking like a lovesick moron. "Something to drink?"

He eyed her warily. "Uh, I'm good."

"I'm getting a glass of wine."

He shrugged. "Fine by me."

I wasn't asking for permission, she wanted to say but didn't. Instead, she smiled at him, left him in the living room and returned with a large glass of red. She fortified her nerves with a sip, then sat on the couch as he continued to loom over her, looking around her house—as if he hadn't already barged in before.

The forty-year-old home suited her—not too big, not too small. She'd designed a garden feature outside, as well as the garden dragons and gnomes to guard her flowers. She'd found most of her furniture through yard sales and flea markets. A few pieces she'd traded for with other artists. A buddy of hers who worked with wood had made her coffee table and side table. She'd also shared some sack time with the guy and enjoyed the fact he knew how to use his hands.

A glance at Dex reminded her that he too was an expert "handyman" as well as having a truly gifted mouth. Jesus. Remembering his wicked tongue, she needed to fan herself. She felt all tingly and drank more wine.

"I didn't see too much of your place the last time I was in here. I like it." He nodded and smiled down at her. "It's you."

"Oh?"

"Yeah. It's artsy but not frilly. Everything is practical yet fun. Totally you."

"Gee. How nice to be called practical. That's right up there with interesting or being called nice."

"Ouch. I only meant I liked your place. Touchy, aren't we?" Instead of sitting next to her on the couch, he took the large chair and sank into it. "Oh wow. This is terrific. I could go to sleep right here."

A spot she often settled into when needing a rest. The thing practically swallowed her friend Ann whole, but for normal or larger-sized people, like her and Dex, the chair was a thing of beauty. "Did you enjoy our *date*?" she asked, gearing up to taunt him into another kiss.

"I did. Even though you tried to sabotage it by inviting your dad and Bev to stick around, I had fun. Learned a lot about you." He put his hands behind his head, the king of the manor.

"Like what?"

"Like you're a pain in the ass to everyone, not just me. Your dad is a hell of a nice guy. Must be sainted after raising you."

"Asshole."

"Wait, I'm not done. I also learned that Bev is a genuinely nice lady. I think she suits your dad."

"She will, but not for long. They never stick with him," she said, shocked to hear a trace of bitterness in her voice. What was that about? She glanced at the wine and moved her glass aside.

"And I learned that you're attracted to me and scared because you like me so much. But then, I always knew that."

Realizing her mouth was open she snapped it shut. "How's that?"

"Well, you invited your dad over to meet me. Obviously we're taking things to the next level. Meet the folks—check."

She rolled her eyes. "I brought him over to save me from you."

"You were so cute and shy, not wanting to hold hands with me where he could see."

"I didn't want to hold hands with you period. Guess what, genius? Dating through blackmail isn't the same as dating because I like you. There's a difference."

"Aha! So you like me."

"I never said that."

"Sounded like it."

"Fuck off."

"You couldn't stop yourself from watching me. Oh yeah, baby. I saw you checking me out at dinner. How you watched me chew up my meager slices of pizza—since you stole the other one." He grinned. "Admit it. You love my mouth."

"When it's frickin' closed," she muttered, wishing she'd stop blushing around the man.

"I'm not done."

"I think you are." She left the couch and launched herself at him.

He caught her with an *oof*, and she straddled him before he could breathe. With her knees on either side of him, her breasts right in his face, she waited for him to make a move.

She watched him swallow—*hard*—and slowly lift his gaze to hers. To his credit, he didn't linger overly on her lips. "Ah, this chair's occupied."

"Is it?" She sat over his lap and ground down against him, not surprised to find him aroused. "Hmm. I'm comfy enough. How about you?" She put her hands on his shoulders and rubbed, then moved to his neck. When she caressed his nape, he shivered, and she smiled.

"Christ. Cut that out. This is a friendly date. No sex. Your rules, remember?"

More than pleased at the lust in his voice, she squirmed over him and felt his hands on her waist. But he didn't push her aside.

"We're friends, aren't we?" *God, his eyes are so pretty.*

"Are we?" he asked. This close, she could see the darker band of gray around his lighter irises. Like a storm warning, his gaze darkened as his body tensed.

She wanted him, no question. And he wanted her. But the jerk wouldn't initiate anything. He sat like a stone, unmoving. She squirmed again and watched his pupils dilate.

"Sure, Dex. We're good friends," she whispered over his lips and kissed him. "Kiss me back," she said against his mouth.

He tried to pull back but she followed him and became the aggressor. Since he wouldn't kiss her, she took charge kissing him. She could feel his bundled energy under her. His grip on her hips would leave marks, but he didn't deepen the kiss, just let her control it with her lips and tongue. God was it sexy.

His moan made it impossible not to ride him—until he stopped her with his hands. He pulled away from her mouth, forced her up on her knees and glared at her. That mean glint turned her arousal from a ten to off-the-charts.

"No sex," he growled.

"Not even a little?" She leaned her chest closer, rubbing against his.

He closed his eyes and swore as she nibbled his bottom lip.

"Fuck, Maya. Back off," came out in a half moan, half snarl as he opened his eyes again.

She smiled and leaned back. "Tell you what, sexy. You ask a question and I'll answer it. That way we'll still get to know each other. But I want a kiss for each answer you get."

"Maya…"

"What? I thought we were friends." She loved being the aggressor, loved too the fact Dex wasn't as in command around her as he wanted to be.

"Fine. But you have to answer honestly."

"Anything you want to know." Then, because she was curious, she added, "And you have to answer me honestly too."

"Yeah, okay. But sit over there—"

"We can't kiss if we're too far apart."

"*Maya…*"

"*Dex…*" She made a face and stole another quick kiss.

He growled when she pulled back, his body vibrating under hers. So much power, so much muscle. She stroked his shoulders and sat on her haunches, which put her directly over his massive erection.

"Why did you freak out about your mom?" Figured he'd ask the question she wanted to answer least right out of the starting gate. "And answer honestly."

She ground against him, enjoying his sensual pain.

"Bastard. You want to know?"

"Yes, damn it."

"You know my mother was Native American."

"Paiute, right?"

She blinked at him. "Um, yeah. Well, she and my dad had a fling. But Dad thought it was more than that. Mom only wanted to get laid. Unfortunately, she had me. I came out a little lighter than she liked, and after suffering with me for a few years, she took off."

His hands were rubbing her hips, then her back. Stroking with comfort in mind, not sexual promise, which she found odd. "Sorry, baby. That sucks."

She shrugged. "I was little so it wasn't a big deal for me. But she broke Dad's heart. He's never been the same. Never been with a woman for more than a year at most. That's why Bev doesn't stand a chance." His relationships had always taken a backseat to raising Maya. Yet even after she'd grown, he still played around, not content to be with one person. Just like her. Not meant to settle down with someone who had the ability to crush you with rejection. What made it worse was that she knew her father could have moved on if he hadn't had to raise Winona Timican's daughter.

"I think maybe it was a big deal to you," Dex said quietly.

She didn't like him asking stupid questions she didn't want to think about, so she rubbed against him, reminding his body what it wanted. "I answered you."

"Honestly?"

"As honest as you're gonna get," she promised. "Now kiss me."

He shocked her by planting a doozy on her. His tongue, lips and teeth took charge until she was a heartbeat away from begging him to fuck. God, with just his mouth he could make her forget every bad thing in her life and concentrate on nothing but feeling good. He was like magic.

Then he yanked himself back and loosened his hold on her hips. To her satisfaction, he must have forgotten his pledge of no sex because he'd been grinding into her something fierce.

"My turn," she said when she could speak.

He cleared his throat and leaned as far back as the cushions would allow.

"Why the blackmail for a date, Dex-ter?" She drawled his name and stroked the back of his neck.

He blinked. She could almost hear the wheels in his mind turning.

She put a finger over his lips. "Uh-uh. Honest answer."

He nipped her, and she ignored the rush of electricity that traveled from her finger to between her legs.

"The truth? I missed you while I was gone and wanted to see if you were still as much a pain in the ass now as you were then." He stared at her with heat in his eyes. "And you are. How's that for honesty?"

"Okay, I guess." He thought she was a pain? Should she be flattered or insulted?

"So why are you so against dating me?"

"Because I don't like you?" Shoot. She'd meant that to be a statement, not a question.

"Try again."

Exasperated, she blew out a breath. "Because dating and I don't mix. I have my friends if I want to hit a movie or do dinner. When I need sex, I find a guy I like and am attracted to. We hit it off, we're happy, we're done. No mess, no fuss."

"Haven't you ever had a serious boyfriend?" He looked fascinated.

She frowned. "A few over the years, and they only reinforced what I know—that I don't do long term. It's too bad I'm not gay, but women do nothing for me sexually. Men do, but they bore me." She stared into his eyes. "It doesn't take long to learn that your gender wants to be catered to and taken care of. Frankly, I have better things to do with my time. I want heavy furniture moved? I can call a moving service. I want sex? I can use a vibrator. So what are you good for?"

"But that's not quality sex." He rubbed her sides. "That's not fucking-against-a-wall, get-your-girl-begging-for-it sex."

She felt her heart race and did her best to relax.

"Come on, baby. Admit you liked feeling me hard and thick inside you," he murmured and pulled her closer. He whispered into her ear, "Remember how good my mouth felt over your clit? How sweet it felt to come over my lips?"

"Dex," she gasped.

Before she could kiss him again, he stood with her in his arms, as if she weighed nothing. He took a step to the side and dumped her on the couch.

"Wh-what?" He withdrew his phone from his back pocket, and the action thrust the prominent bulge in his jeans into relief. She wanted to taste him so badly.

"What's that?" he said into the phone, his voice thick as he stared down at her. "Really? A plumbing emergency? Right now? Okay." He ended the call and moved to her front door. Without turning around, he said, "Sorry, Maya. Gotta go. Anson needs me. I'll text you for our next date. Bye." And he was gone.

She sat there, sexually frustrated, confused and annoyed at how he'd gotten her so hot so fast, then literally dumped her on her ass.

"Friggin' Dexter Black."

She fumed long into the night and right into the next morning. Had he really had an emergency to attend to? If so, why hadn't he asked her to drop him off? Granted, the walk to Anson's restaurant—if that's where he'd gone—wasn't too far. But for an emergency, wouldn't he want speed?

After breakfast, she did some preliminary sketches for a few pieces she intended to make for some upcoming art shows. Winter time brought good money, and people liked local wares. After spending her morning vacillating between believing and disbelieving Dex and wishing she had the energy to go grocery shopping, she put her sketchbook away and walked the few blocks to Riley's bakery for something to eat.

On the way, she passed the construction crew working on Anson's new place. The small cottage-turned-restaurant had charm, and she imagined if he did it right and put a great chef in place, he'd make a lot of money. Rumor had it everything the annoying man touched turned to gold. His name had been in the newspaper many times over the years to note the successes of a good old local boy. She knew because Riley helpfully pointed out the arrogant ass's accomplishments with both pride and annoyance. Weird, and a very Riley thing to do. God forbid she simply hate the guy.

"Hey, baby," one of the workers called and waved. "Nice boots."

She laughed. She'd worn a short skirt and knee-high leather boots showing a good bit of skin. Having a man compliment her, without sounding crass, put a smile on her face. "Thanks." She waved. He held his heart and swooned, and a few of his friends leaned out of open windows to shout friendly greetings.

"Get back to work," she heard Anson bark. "What the hell?" The men disappeared, and then Anson stuck his head out the window. "Should have known."

"Well, hey there, Anson. How's it hanging?" she yelled and heard laughter from inside.

"Just great, thanks." He sounded less than enthused to see her.

"How's your water leak?"

He frowned. "My what?"

I knew it. Dex, that lying coward. A part of her reveled in the fact that the man had been forced to lie to escape her dastardly clutches, while the other part was pissed she'd missed out on naked Dexter in a chair.

"You know. Dex left last night to help you with that water leak? And something about a small fire?" She tacked that on for fun, baiting the hook.

"Oh, right." He didn't so much as blink as he lied. "The leak. We're good."

"And the fire?"

"Not a problem. Thanks for asking." He ducked back inside before she could put his feet to the fire—so to speak.

Now she had a bone to pick with Dex, and she couldn't wait to make him pay for fibbing. Most women would probably be annoyed, maybe even hurt. Maya wanted to pump her fist in victory. She'd scared him. Big bad Dex Black, scared of a little old artist.

Breezing into Riley's bakery, she stopped and inhaled with pleasure. The small shop had several tables currently occupied by people munching on cupcakes, tarts and fritters. Maya's mouth watered. Screw grocery shopping. She planned on making a meal out of something totally not good for her.

"Can I help you?" Dina, the perky teenager behind the counter, asked.

"Yeah, is the cranky perfectionist who practically lives in the back here?"

Dina grinned and yelled over her shoulder, "Riley, someone's here for you."

Maya chuckled, especially when Riley came out with flour on her cheek and a harried expression on her face. "Oh. It's you." She darted back into her cooking cave, as Maya liked to call it.

More people entered the shop, taking up Dina's attention

while Maya followed Riley into the back. She skirted two other bakers and sought her friend.

Maya leaned back against the one empty counter not covered in confections. "You look like crap."

"Thanks." Riley glared at her. "Is it my lucky day or do you actually need something?" She concentrated on some candy toppings for the cupcakes. What looked like little happy faces wearing glasses. Damn, the girl was good.

"That is so cool." Maya leaned closer and Riley pushed her back with an elbow.

"You're blocking my light. What do you need?"

"Someone to talk to." Maya glanced around, then snagged a cupcake. "And a vanilla cupcake."

"Hey." Riley frowned.

"Oh relax, tight ass. Put it on my tab."

"Don't think I won't," Riley grumbled. "Can you believe this? My best customer forgets the cake for her kid's birthday, so I have to make twenty cupcakes in like fifteen minutes. What the hell?"

"But she's your best customer," Maya said for her. "And you don't want to piss her off."

"No." Riley sighed and wiped her forehead with the short sleeve of her pink tee-shirt.

"How is it that even sweaty and harassed, you look like a model? That's really annoying."

Riley smirked. "Sorry, Maya. I don't swing that way."

"You wish. I'm strictly dickly."

Riley snickered with her as she continued to work. "Okay, so why are you here using up my oxygen?"

Maya told her about her date with Dex, which brought a grin to her friend's face. "You're kidding. He made up a fake emergency to get out with his pants on? That's classic."

"Thanks so much. It's not like I was going to molest the guy. Much." Just enough for an orgasm or two. "I might have said something about us not having sex while dating, but that was before we actually had sex."

"And you found out he's a stud in bed," Riley guessed.

"Yeah. Now he's got this hang-up about no sex while we're dating—and we only have eight left. I have no clue how to deal with him."

"Well, if it were me, I'd be rushing over to help him with his water leak. The poor guy is probably ass-deep in rusty pipes."

"Not to mention a pretend fire I made up that Anson corroborated."

"Anson." Riley frowned.

Maya chewed her cupcake, in love as always with Riley's recipes.

"Why are you still here? Go get Dex." Riley set one piping bag down, picked up another and started frosting chocolate cupcakes like mad. Then she set the candy decorations in the middle of each one and finally transferred them into a large box. She called to one of her assistants. "Tim, have Dina phone Jean, would you?" She handed him the box.

He nodded and left with it.

She sighed. "Jean has recommended so many people to me it's not funny. I guess a rush on some cupcakes is no big deal in the long run."

"Yeah, yeah, I get it. Cupcakes, check. Back to me, Riley. What did you mean by go get Dex?"

Riley rubbed her back and stretched. Maya winced, hearing something pop.

"Oh, that's better," Riley purred. "So Dex has the hots for you. He's scared he has no control when he's with you, and he totally wussed out last night. But you want him? Go get him. Go, and I quote, 'help him out' with his leak. And I do mean help him." Riley grabbed an order pad and scribbled down the address.

"How do you know where he lives?" Maya did her best not to sound jealous.

Riley busied herself cleaning up the table near her. "Oh, well, Anson lives with Dex, and he made sure I had his address in case I had any problems with the construction next door."

Maya blinked. "Really? Not his phone number to call him, but his address?"

"He said he doesn't have a phone installed yet."

"What, no cell phone?"

Riley looked up and scowled.

Maya could see the woman blushing. "Ha! You are so in for it. Wait until I tell Ann—"

"I gave you sound advice," Riley interrupted. "You tell Ann nothing! She's a blabbermouth with Jack, and I don't want him telling Anson *anything*. Not that there's anything to tell."

Maya nodded, doing her best not to laugh. "Um, sure. Nothing to tell. Thanks for the address." She tore off the page from the pad. "Well then. See you later tonight, right? Just us or will Ann be there too?"

"She'll be there. I already guilted her about valuing her vagina over us. I mean, sex with Jack, or whining and wine with the girls?"

Maya agreed. "Us, no contest." She slapped Riley on the back then turned to leave. "Wish me luck."

"Better yet, I'll wish Dex luck. When you get that look in your eye, I pity the guy on the receiving end."

Chapter Seven

Maya walked to the address Riley had given her, not surprised to find Dex and Anson's home in much better shape than her own and in a good neighborhood. Like hers, the neighborhood was eclectic. Nice houses sat near crappy ones, but it made for an interesting community.

She walked up the stairs of his porch and knocked. "Dex?"

Nothing. She raised her hand to knock again, then stopped. If he could just walk into her place, surely she could do the same. She turned the knob, and to her pleasant surprise, it opened.

With a grin, she let herself inside and locked it behind her. A moment of silence convinced her he wasn't at home, until she stepped deeper into the house and heard the faint sound of a shower.

She glanced at a clock on the wall. Twelve in the afternoon and he was taking a shower? Whatever.

His place was only slightly less messy than hers. A few magazines, some beer bottles and dishes had been scattered across several tables. A thin layer of dust covered most of the wooden furniture. But the rest of the place seemed nice. Not exactly a bachelor pad where one's feet stuck to the floor. Still, it didn't have any personality beyond the small clutter. The man needed some color, or at least a few photographs or pictures. Ironic that such an ace photographer had nothing on his own walls.

She followed the sound of the shower up the stairs and down a hallway, passing two doors. Maya had no right letting herself into his home and invading his privacy, but God love her, she couldn't deny herself the possible sight of Dex covered in nothing but soap and water.

She knocked on the bathroom door as she opened it. "Hey, Dex. It's me."

"*Shit*," came from behind the striped shower curtain. "I'm in the shower."

"Duh."

"Privacy?"

"Yeah, you'd think you'd have some, in the shower and all." She chuckled. "Guess you're right about leaving your front door unlocked. I mean, just *anyone* can come walking into your home. Or your bathroom." She took a step closer to the large stall.

"Don't even think of opening the curtain," he warned.

"What was that? Open the curtain? Your shower is awfully loud." She toed off her boots and tore off her clothes, naked in seconds.

"Maya?"

She stepped inside the stall. His body blocked the water, giving her an up-close look at six feet four inches of wet, muscular Dexter Black.

"Oh man. Not naked." He reached for her, only to be held at bay by Maya's hand.

"Nope. You owe me for being such a bad liar." She let him

look his fill, saw the way he tensed. There was no mistaking the erection pointed in her direction either.

"I don't know what you're talking about."

"Oh?" She spread her legs and dragged a hand over her body, cupping her breasts, teasing her pussy, her thighs. "So how's that water leak treating you?"

"Hmm." He took a step closer.

"Next time clue your cousin in to your lies or you'll give yourself away."

"Cousin. Sure." He moved to kiss her, but she planted a hand on his chest again.

"Uh-uh. You owe me." She tugged his shoulder, urging him to kneel. Smart guy that he was, he didn't fight her. He knelt and ran his hands over her legs, her ass, her hips…

"Spread for me," he ordered.

His blatant desire only aroused her more. She widened her stance, and he kissed her right there, between her legs. His tongue stroked her toward orgasm, his intensity and focus on consuming her more than she could handle. The water continued to rain over his back, and she cupped his wet hair, perilously close to coming.

He thrust a thick finger inside her and sucked harder, and she came embarrassingly fast. But Dex wouldn't stop. He moaned her name against her flesh, continuing to lick and pump his finger. Then he added another before withdrawing them, and she thought she was done.

Breathing hard, her hands still clenched in his hair, her knees trembling, she watched him with an affection growing into something more. Something dangerous, unstable and real. Something that refused to go away. With every kiss, he dug deeper under her emotional shields, and she didn't know what to do about it.

"You are fucking beautiful when you come," he said. "I could eat you all the time. So sweet." He stood, and she thought he meant to kiss her. Instead, he turned her to face the wall while the hot water hit her side. The added stimulation made her shudder.

"Yeah, stand just like that. Don't move." He ran his hands over her back and ass, then stepped closer, putting that fat cock between her cheeks. He held himself there a moment, then slid, rubbing against her. "You have any idea what I want to do to you? How much you need my discipline?"

"D-discipline?" Hell, she was still trying to get her breath back from coming so hard.

"Yeah. You need to be spanked. Tied up. Ass-fucked and gagged on my cock until you realize where you belong."

She couldn't move, caught in the lustful fantasy he wove around her without even trying. Dex was one kinky bastard, and she felt as if she'd stepped into heaven. "Where I *what*?" she said when she could speak.

"Where you belong." He knelt behind her and pried her buttocks wide. "Beneath me," he added before sliding the tip of his finger against her ass.

• • •

Dex ached to be inside her. *Shit.* Eating her out after dreaming about her all night long had only prolonged his frustration. No way he could stop himself from having her, not when she'd gotten naked and confronted him in his own fucking shower. And he'd been doing so well not jacking off—*again*—to the memories of doing her in his studio.

Now he planned to make good on his promises. Some good old-fashioned discipline might steer the woman in the right direction. Even better, this technically wasn't a date. She'd come to him and they sure as hell weren't getting to know each other through conversation. Though he wanted to wait and continue to court her, he couldn't deny either of them the pleasure they both craved.

"Dex, God. What are you doing to me?"

"You like this?" He eased his finger around her hole, rimming her before dipping the tip inside her. "'Cause I am dying to fuck you here. Come on, admit it. You like a little kink."

She moaned. "So what if I do?"

Oh yeah. She totally fit him, like a lock and key. "So I'm thinking I have the house to myself for once. You're here, naked. I'm still hard and hurting."

"Oh?"

He huffed. "Fine. Yeah, I lied last night. But you pushed me into it by trying to turn our date into a hookup."

She snickered, and he wanted to get down on one knee and beg her to marry him. She was sexy, a little mean, and so affectionate when he stroked her just right. Like taming a feral cat, she only needed the right petting to bring out her loving side. He wanted that more than anything. For Maya to give him what only he should have a right to take—her heart.

But first, he'd take control of her body. Because he was right. She needed it.

"What are you going to do to me, Dex?"

He continued to caress her ass, playing with the water and using it to ease the slight penetration of his finger. The woman gripped him like a vise, and he swallowed a groan. "I'm going to own you, baby."

She looked over her shoulder at him. "You think you can handle me?"

He stood and leaned into her so she could feel all of him. "I *know* I can handle you."

"Oh?"

He gripped his cock. "Get on your knees. I think it's time you showed me what else that mouth is good for."

"Dick." She frowned at him and turned around.

"My thoughts exactly."

She blinked then smirked at him. "You're the king of bad puns."

"No, I'm the king of sexually frustrated. Now get on your fucking knees and blow me." He gripped her by the hair. Not the most romantic of declarations, but by the way she maintained eye contact and practically melted at his feet, he knew he'd found the right way to connect with her.

"So bossy," she breathed.

"That's right. Now open up and take me in." He stared, unable to look away, as she parted her lips and enveloped his cockhead.

She took his hand away from the root of his shaft and eased her mouth over him, taking him deeper.

"Fuck, Maya. That's good," he could barely get out as she found a rhythm that threatened to take him out of this world. She bobbed over him and cupped his balls, drawing her skillful tongue over his shaft like it was a fucking lollipop.

He hissed and moaned, tangled his hands in her hair and couldn't look away.

His dreams of her sucking him off had never come close to the reality. Especially because she'd closed her eyes and was making soft noises while she pleasured him. She looked enraptured, as into the scene as he was, and her honest desire made everything so much better.

"I'm gonna come, baby. You might want to pull back..." he tried to warn her.

Maya clenched his ass and gagged herself on him, taking him to the back of her throat. Then she did something with her tongue and teeth that shot him over the edge.

"*Fuck,*" he swore as he came, unable to hold back. He pumped a few times, releasing so hard he feared he'd pass out.

When he could function again, Maya finished swallowing

him, pulled away and stood. She stroked his chest and arms, then drew his face down for a kiss. He eased into her, bemused at her tenderness. Then, because he had to, he assumed control of the embrace and pulled her into his arms.

He didn't move away until they were both gasping for air. And damn if she hadn't gotten him half-hard again. "You rock my world, Maya Werner."

She smiled, and the beauty in her joy was contagious. "You're not so bad yourself, Dexter Black."

"But we're not done." He ran his hands up her body and cupped her breasts, then pinched her nipples, making her gasp. "Not yet. Time to put you through your paces, hmm? Give you some real Dex lovin'."

She bit her lower lip, and he wanted her to suck him off all over again. She had the plumpest, ripest mouth. "Just what do you have in mind, studly?"

• • •

Maya laid naked, spread-eagle on his king-size bed, her wrists tied above her head, her legs wide because she'd been ordered to keep them that way.

Dex knelt between her thighs with a look of concentration. He'd always worn that look when engaged in something geeky back in high school. But now, his focus remained on her, and *geeky* didn't come close to describing the sexy, handsome giant playing her body like an instrument.

"You have a big cock," she teased, breathless and wanting him the same.

Dex looked cool and in control. Only his erection confirmed he felt anything lusty toward her at the moment.

"Yeah, and it's hard for you. I've got stamina, be warned." He gave her a mean smile, and she shivered. "I know we need condoms, and I'm okay with that for now. But I want you to know I'm clean. I haven't been with anyone in a long while and I always use protection."

"Um, right. Me too."

"Good." His smile widened. "So then if we're both clean, and we're only using the condoms to prevent any Dex Juniors from arriving nine months from now, then I shouldn't need to wear one when I'm buried up your ass, should I?"

"*What?*" The word came out in an embarrassing squeak. She tugged at her bonds. The tight restraints reinforced her helplessness. And fuelled her lust.

"You can't go anywhere unless I let you go. And I'm not planning on doing that anytime soon. This is for your own good, Maya."

"You bully."

He shook his head, a playful glint in his gaze. "We both know you need a strong man to take you in hand. Time to show you I'm the guy you've been waiting for."

So arrogant, yet that confidence captivated her. Best not to be too easy about it though. She tossed her head on the pillow. "Yeah? Prove it."

"I'm not gonna wear a condom," he reminded her.

"We'll see if you're worth it," she caged, not committing to a yes or no.

He smiled. "I'll have you begging."

If only... How long had it been since Maya had been more than just pleased by a lover? Already with Dex she'd been out of her mind with desire. If he could continue his stellar record, she'd almost want to marry him—if she were the marrying kind, which she wasn't.

"Bring it, Poindexter."

He stunned her by slapping her pussy. The slight sting should have hurt, but it didn't. The sudden smack shot heat through her core. "You're a brat. But then, you always have been." He slapped her twice more, short, firm pressure over her bursting clit that stung but didn't cause lasting pain. The shocking pleasure confused her.

"Dex?"

He tapped her again, and she bucked off the bed. "I knew you'd be into this." He kissed her before she could ask him what he meant. A hard, punishing kiss that ended with a bite on her lip.

"You *bit* me." Dexter Black was into all kinds of kink, apparently. She blinked up at him, stunned and turned on anew.

"Because I own you." He scooted up her body, straddled her neck and angled his cock at her lips. "Suck me. Now."

She opened her mouth, loving the commanding side of the normally mellow guy.

"Don't stop until I tell you to."

She let him thrust deeper, pumping inside her. Sometimes he stole her breath, and sometimes he withdrew until only the tip of his cockhead stayed between her lips.

"Enough," he said, his voice thick. He pulled back before lowering himself over her mouth again. "Now suck my balls."

Kinky bastard, was all she could think as she laved him with loving attention, noting the hard knots signaling his rise toward climax.

"Jesus, I love your mouth."

She sucked one ball into her mouth and he jerked. He left her and scooted down her body again. While he trailed his mouth from her neck to her breasts, he continued to pet her. Soothing her with easy strokes of his rough hands. Then the sexual dictator gave no warning. He bit one nipple while pinching the other hard enough to hurt.

She arched into the pain even as he relented by sucking the sting away from first one breast, then the other. Then he did it again, nipping and pinching before kissing her all better.

The fire between her legs roared, her need for him

increasing in urgency. "Dex, in me. Now."

"Not yet. Not until you're so wet for me you can't stand it."

"I'm wet now."

"Are you?" He scooted down her body and shoved a finger inside her. "A little bit."

Was he crazy? She felt super slick.

Then his mouth found her clit, and she moaned his name as he licked and sucked her while playing with her until she wanted to scream. He'd bring her close, then back off. Then take her to the edge of orgasm before easing away again.

"Dex, *fuck me already.*"

He rose over her to blanket her body, his so much larger. Leaning over her, he stared into her eyes. "Don't you get it? You don't give the orders here. *I* do." He shook his head. "Guess I need to remind you I'm in charge."

He kissed her—soft and easy—and she found herself surrendering into his keeping. Especially when he nudged his cock against her clit. He rocked against her a few times, and she thought she was ready for him.

But when he thrust the whole of him inside her in one great big push, she felt too full, invaded, stretched.

"Shit. So good," he rasped as he fucked her. Nothing gentle or easy about him now, but a rough taking that brought her to orgasm in an instant.

She cried his name as she clamped around him. The belated thought he hadn't worn a condom penetrated, but by then he'd already withdrawn.

He reached past her to his nightstand and knelt between her legs. She roused enough to see him drizzling lube over his cock. "Time to take that fine ass," he rumbled, and she nodded, caught under his spell. "Open for me."

She spread her legs wider, letting him prop her hips up on a pillow. He liberally coated a finger with lube and pushed it inside her ass. Watching her while he played with her, he kept asking how she felt, if it was too much or not enough.

After some time, she admitted, "It doesn't hurt anymore," stunned to experience such pleasure and fullness when before she'd felt nothing but discomfort. Her short forays into anal sex had not been fun. But this… She felt as if she'd fallen into an adult three-ring circus with Dex playing ringmaster.

"I need you. Gotta have you." He sounded guttural, and the intensity on his face shook her.

Had she ever been watched with such hunger, such lust? Had anyone ever taken such care with her before? For all that he'd been rough and aggressive, he continued to study how she felt. He asked her questions, watched her, and now as he readied to put himself inside her ass, he moved slowly, with deliberate intent to take and give pleasure.

"In me, Dex. Please," she whispered, staring into his dark eyes.

He didn't smile or laugh as he withdrew and positioned himself. Even slick, his cock was much larger than his finger. He moved slowly, easing into her.

"Relax. Take me in, baby," he said, moving in increments. "Oh fuck. That's it. Let me…yeah." He continued to move inside her, patiently stopping to allow her to adjust, until all of him penetrated.

She'd never had anal sex while facing her partner, and having him watch her while he buried himself deep was off-putting—because it felt more intimate than she could have imagined.

"I want all of you, Maya." He pulled out a fraction then surged deeper. Watching her while he fucked her, he thrust the whole of himself in and out of her, taking care with slow, thorough movements.

His arms and chest looked huge while he braced himself above her. His stomach muscles contracted with each pass, and she glanced down, seeing where he ended and she began.

Connected together.

"I have to move faster," he groaned. "You're so fucking hot." Dex increased his pace. The fullness felt so right, and his looming orgasm spurred her toward another. While he continued to pump inside her, he moved a hand between them to rub her clit.

She jolted, sending him deeper inside her. They both moaned before she confessed, "I'm close, Dex."

He closed his eyes, then opened them, the naked lust in his expression overwhelming. "Come with me, Maya. Be with me."

He rubbed harder, and when she tensed in climax, he let her go to pound inside her until he too jerked and came. He said her name as he spent, and his expression verged on primal. She wanted to capture *him* on film, to see him like that again. And again. And maybe once more…

When he finally started to soften, he gently withdrew. He left the bed and returned to clean her up. After taking care of her, he removed her restraints and tucked her into his body, curling around her like a giant purring tiger.

They lay with each other, not speaking, just breathing and trying to adjust to the pleasure still making them weak.

Then Dex, being Dex, had to say, "For the record, this wasn't a date."

She wished she had the energy to laugh. He'd thoroughly worn her out. "What would you call it?"

"A little piece of heaven." He sighed and hugged her tight. "Give me a half hour and we'll go again."

"Seriously?" She wanted to nap and not wake up until next week.

"Please. We have yet to do some reverse cowgirl or even sixty-nine. I have standards, woman."

She let out a sigh. "The things I do for lust."

"You're damn straight."

Chapter Eight

"So." Ann stared at Maya that evening as they sat on Riley's couch. Whine and Wine night had apparently gone by the wayside in favor of Let's Make Maya Uncomfortable night.

"So," Riley mimicked Ann's tone. "Seems to me like you were walking funny when you came in."

Maya tried to hide behind her hands.

Riley pulled them away. "He used and abused you, didn't he? That dirty Dex."

"You're such a whore," Ann said in that sweet voice that always sounded hilarious when used with coarse language.

"I know." Maya wanted to sound more dejected, but her chipper answer spoke volumes.

"Ah-ha!" Riley smiled. "I knew it. You like him."

"Yep, she does." Great. Ann knew. Now she'd tell Jack.

"You can't tell Jack," Maya warned. "He'll tell Dex and Anson."

Riley exchanged a glance with Ann. "Um, Maya? I think Dex already knows you like him. Otherwise, why would you now be bowlegged?"

"Shut up." She groaned. "That man seriously rang my bell. How the hell am I going to get back at him now? He has all the power." And part of her loved that about him.

"You aren't seriously still stuck on our stupid revenge pledge, are you?" Ann shook her head. "We're striving to be mature women here. Not high school girls with a bug up our collective asses."

"Ouch." Riley grimaced. "That hurt."

"Dex is a sweetheart who seriously likes you," Ann continued. "Go with it. You could—and have—done much worse."

"True, you have," Riley agreed. "Remember Dan? Mike? How about Frank? Ugh. What a loser."

"He had a nice car."

"You mean *his mom* had a nice car she let him drive," Riley corrected.

Ann nodded. "Oh, right. Frank. Big dick, but a momma's boy."

Riley cringed. "Ew. Don't say dick and momma in the same sentence. That's just wrong."

"*My point,*" Ann interrupted, "is that Dex is the first decent guy you've dated in a long time."

"Not dating. Just having sex with," Maya felt the need to correct. "We're not dating…exactly. Blackmail, remember?"

"Whatever you call it," Riley said. "It's working. Don't screw it up. He seems to tolerate your moods and actually likes you for more than your breasts."

Maya frowned, ignoring the breasts remark. Though she did concede that she had a nice set. "It's funny, but there hasn't been that much awfulness to tolerate. I don't think I've been in a bad mood with him. Weird."

"Not weird. He makes you happy. You've been smiling more since Dex has been around than you have this past decade," Ann said drily. "Go with it. What can being with

Dex hurt?"

"Um, hello? Any of you met my father? The man with the broken heart who hasn't moved on in thirty years? Werners aren't lucky when it comes to love."

"You're still using your dad as an excuse? How lame." Riley snorted. "Even for you that's stretching things. You like Dex. Don't be such a wuss. Bitch up." One of Ann's more colorful phrases, which Riley seemed to have adopted. "You don't have to marry him, for God's sake. Enjoying the man's company isn't wrong, and it just might help you get that closure you think you still need."

"And you don't?"

"Anson is a different thing entirely." Riley looked at Ann, who nodded her support. "He's a competitive asshole who needs to be kicked down a peg or ten. Dex is nice, studly, and according to you, killer-good in bed. What's not to like?"

"He could break my heart." A pitiful defense, but it was all she had left. Dex was too charming and amazing in bed to resist.

Riley moved closer and pulled Maya into a hug—then shifted her around and turned it into a headlock.

"Ow, *damn it*."

Riley increased the pressure around Maya's neck while Ann laughed. "If he breaks your heart, we'll break him. Right, Ann?"

"Right. I'll make Jack tear off his arms and legs, then we'll shove them down his throat."

Maya rasped, "Aren't you a little too bloodthirsty to be teaching second grade?" She coughed when Riley laughed and tightened her hold. "Riley, get off."

"I will, but only if you tell us all about Dex's antics in bed. Some of us only have gingerbread men in our lives, you know?"

Finally, the woman eased up. Maya shoved her arm away.

"Just for that, I'm not going to sugarcoat his skills to make you feel any better."

"Bitch." Riley groaned. "Tell us."

"You asked for it. He's *amazing* in bed. Kinky, dominating, and *way* more than six inches. His mother should have named him Studly McCocks-A-Lot, because he's *never* tired."

"I think I hate you," Riley muttered.

"Me too. And I have Jack." Ann tried to look sad, then blew it by laughing. "How about his O face? Hot or not?"

Maya frowned. Yep, even in orgasm, the man was smokin'. "Totally hot. Do you know how hard it is to find something I don't like about the guy? I have to make shit up. That's downright annoying."

"Well, if you need a list of bad traits to look for, I could list a bunch of Anson's for you," Riley offered. "Some of it's bound to be genetic."

Ann nodded. "Sounds good. Then I'll tell you how aggravating Jack can be when he, ah... Well, he stacks his clean socks and leaves them on the dresser for longer than I'd like. Although he does put them away before bed. But we're only newly sleeping at each other's places, so he might get neater and more annoying." At Riley's look, she nodded. "I'm sure he will."

"I hate you too," Riley said.

Maya grinned with Ann, feeling a kinship with the petite redhead. They had found happiness with their...men. *God, Dex feels like my man. When the hell did that happen?*

"...Riley. Get Anson off your chest," Ann was saying.

Which was likely where the guy wanted to be—on or near Riley's chest. Anson might not like her, but even Maya could see the way the guy lusted after Riley's body.

Thinking about lust reminded her of Dex, and despite trying to keep her thoughts and emotions centered around her friends, she wondered what her tall goofy photographer was up to—unable to stop herself from wishing he sat next to her right now.

• • •

Friday night they had their third date at a game center that normally catered to kids. Adults gathered too, so Dex didn't feel too out of place. There were some arcade games, bowling, an outdoor batting cage, go-karts and miniature golf—the sport Maya had chosen to "wipe the floor" with him. The night had been going well until he suggested they up their stakes from bragging rights to sexual favors. He couldn't help it. His competitive nature insisted he up the ante, especially since he'd been beating her all night long. After losing to him a second time, Maya called him a few choice names and took a soda break.

Grumbling the whole while, she ignored him as she guzzled down some sugar water. Honestly, the woman should have been majorly buzzed after two candy bars and three sodas. But somehow she regulated her intake of sugar and caffeine. More than one cup of coffee for Dex and he was jazzed for hours.

Just as they turned in their putters, Dex noticed a sight he could have done without—Selena Thorpe surrounded by several town council members and her trust-fund friends. He knew several of them from high school. They'd been jerks back then. He couldn't imagine they'd gotten any better.

Blond, beautiful and loaded after having bled husband number three for as much as she could, the surgically sculpted Selena saw him and smiled. When she noticed Maya, her smile grew wider, but a lot less pleasant.

Shit.

Maya finished her drink and tossed it in the trash. She hadn't seen Selena yet. Perhaps Dex could salvage the evening by taking her as far away as possible.

"Oh, Dex-ter. Dex?" Selena sauntered over to them while her friends watched from a distance, crowding near the batting cages.

Maya stiffened, her back still to the woman. "That voice. The voice of *evil*." She turned. "What the hell is *she* doing here? Looking for a four-year-old to fleece after foregoing another prenup?"

He held his laughter. Encouraging Maya wouldn't be good. The last time she and Selena met, Maya had busted her nose. It had been so satisfying to see Selena go down, yet he'd been scared for Maya as well. In this day and age, a simple fistfight could turn into assault and battery and lawsuits. A good thing Anson had talked the woman down from filing *more* charges. The only thing standing between Maya and jail had been Dex's reluctance to support Selena's account of what had transpired between them, and Anson's silence, for which he still owed his cousin a huge favor.

Here there would be way too many witnesses to ignore.

"How are you, handsome?" Selena asked as she came abreast of them. She hadn't been too impressed with him when they'd met two weeks ago. Then she'd heard of his financial success, and suddenly he was no longer that unpopular geek from high school.

"Hello, Selena." He'd talk his way out of a possible altercation with manners. "You remember Maya." He took a firm hold of Maya's hand, refusing to let go. He'd learned his lesson.

"I'm sure her nose does," Maya said with a smirk.

Selena's blue eyes narrowed over her bruised nose. Too bad she was such a viper. He would have loved to shoot her portrait. "You little bitch. Don't worry, I'll keep my distance. Wouldn't want to get *scalped*." Selena tittered.

He felt Maya tense, knew she'd been teased about her

heritage growing up and wondered if she still had to tolerate such nonsense from people—other than Selena. In this day and age, he wouldn't think the PC-crowd could be so crass.

"Got my tomahawk in my back pocket. Best watch your step or I'll yank off a patch of your bottle-blonde hair." Maya's smile would have looked at home on a shark.

He winced. "Ah, we'd better get going."

"You sure?" Selena stepped closer to him. "I feel bad for you, keeping company with such trash. A girl like Maya, you don't know where she's been." She flicked Maya a contemptuous glance. "But then, you always were a Boy Scout. Helping those less fortunate and fundraising for the chess club. I admire that."

"Photography club, actually," he muttered.

Selena smiled. "You're such a good man, Dex. I'll see you around." She turned and strutted away, rejoining the snobs he recognized and wished he didn't.

Maya took a step after her so Dex tightened his grip.

"Easy, killer. Let her go. We don't need trouble."

"From her?" Maya snorted. "Only trouble she has is keeping her legs and mouth closed. See? They're still open."

He deliberately turned them away from Selena and walked in the other direction. "I won the game. We're done here."

"Lucky shot."

"*Twice.* So let's leave. Can I interest you in—"

"More sex? Sure."

He flushed when an older woman looked his way at the comment. To Maya, he whispered, "Keep your voice down."

Maya snickered. "Selena's a bitch, but she's right about one thing. You are a Boy Scout." She ripped her hand away from his and latched onto his arm. "So when are you going to heat up my sheets again?"

They'd been together Wednesday and Thursday, and

they would have been together today too if this hadn't been a date. He refused to let her dictate what they did all the time. Dates, in his opinion, were for getting to know each other. Not for fucking until they couldn't breathe.

They hadn't been together for that long, but he swore he was wearing her down. She smiled at him. A lot. Not making fun, but *having* fun. A big difference.

"I want to shoot you," he said as they left the fun center.

"Well gee, maybe if you promise to use a .22 and aim for the fleshy part of my arm, so it doesn't hurt too much."

"Smart ass." He held open the door of his truck for her, then got in and headed out of the parking lot. "I meant I want to take your picture. Will you pose for me?"

"Hmm. Maybe. What do I get if I do?"

"What do you want?" She just grinned at him. Dumb question. "Is sex all you ever think about?"

"With that cock of yours so near me, yeah."

Of course he had a hard-on. He always did around her. He adjusted himself and concentrated on the road. "Our dates are for getting to know each other with our clothes on."

"All I'm hearing from you is no sex." She sighed. "But okay, I'll play. Tell me about your parents."

"What's to tell? Only child of Connie and Theo Black. Nice people."

"Rich people," she corrected. "How come you're not as obnoxious as Selena and her cronies?"

He shrugged. "Money isn't the same thing to everyone. To my mom and dad, it's a means of securing our family's future. They live in a nice, normal house. They have two cars, one for each of them. And okay, my dad's is a Mercedes, but my mom drives a Hyundai."

She grinned. "Not a Lexus?"

He shook his head.

"What do they think of you doing Pocahontas?" What

kids had once called her in school.

"My parents don't see color, Maya."

"I hate to break it to you, Boy Scout, but everyone does."

"They don't care about it. Not like I do. Yeah, I'm totally prejudiced. I'm only into darker-skinned women with dusky nipples and a smooth pussy that tastes like—"

"Would you stop?" she snapped.

"Embarrassed?" He chuckled. "I thought you had a healthy sex drive and weren't afraid to say so. Women who have sex aren't slutty, you said. They're empowered feminists. I agree, by the way. Which is why we'll be fucking first thing in the morning, after we wake up. A new day, not a date day."

That had her attention. "Excuse me?"

"This is date number three. And like you said at the very beginning of our relationship—"

"Blackmailed association."

"—we can't have sex. Because then I'd technically be blackmailing you into it. And paying to get between your legs is like prostitution. That's what you said before."

"Not exactly," she hedged.

"Close enough. I have to draw a line somewhere."

"God forbid you do a bad thing," she muttered.

"Exactly. But interesting that you neatly diverted us from talking about *you*. You do that a lot. Ask me a bazillion questions about what I like and do, but you don't share much about yourself."

He shifted in his seat. He actually disliked talking about himself. Dex had always been on the shy side, only losing most of that when he grew into his size-thirteen feet after high school. It would probably amuse her to know he still occasionally felt tongue-tied around her. Looking into her beautiful brown eyes could leave him mute with appreciation. She had beauty that went soul deep.

"You want us to get to know each other?" said Maya.

"Well, that includes me asking questions. That's not deflecting. That's me being curious."

That had to be a good thing, right? He felt her gaze like a caress and swallowed a sigh.

She asked, "Do you get along with your parents?" Still wanting to know about his parents.

"Yes."

"Really well or just tolerably?"

"Like you and your dad. We're close."

She nodded. "You and Anson still tight?"

"Yep. Jack too. It's like we never left Bend." The three of them had been gone for twelve years and had come back in the span of a few months. It felt like they'd always been together. Some friends were just like that.

"Hurray for assholes sticking together."

He grinned. "You do know that your attitude does nothing but make me hard."

"And we're back to sex." She sighed. "I take back everything I said before. Now why can't we go back to my place and fuck like bunnies? Because I don't understand. We can still be 'friendly' when you're buried inside me."

He gritted his teeth. "Do you *have* to say things like that?"

"Oh, baby. I surely do." She licked her lips, and he groaned. She laughed. "So what's your favorite thing to do to me?"

"I have to pick just one?"

"Yeah."

"I can't," he said. "I like it all."

She quieted, and he chanced a glance at her, only to see her studying him.

"What?" he asked when she remained quiet.

"Would your mom like me?"

"Well that killed the mood." He blew out a breath. "Of

course she'd like you. You're beautiful, smart, obnoxious, and you're an artist. My mom has a soft spot for artists."

"Oh. Is she into art?"

"My grandfather—her dad—was a starving painter. Great talent, not so good at marketing himself. She's always been more than supportive of my photography."

"That's good."

"What about you? Did your dad always support you?"

It amazed him how pleasant and unguarded she could seem when she let herself just be with him.

She nodded. "I've always been into doing my own thing. Pottery was a natural extension of expressing myself. Dad has always been there for me." She grew quiet. "He's the only one, other than Ann or Riley, who I can count on."

Too soon to tell her, *You can count on me.* So he changed the subject again. "Where should we go on date number four?"

"My bed?"

"No, seriously."

She grinned. "I am serious."

He expelled a frustrated breath. "So far, our dates have given me some pretty deep insights into your life. I already know what sex with you is like."

"We went to a restaurant, had pizza and golfed. Exactly what do you think you know about me?"

"Besides knowing you're a dynamo in bed, I know you're competitive. You have a hot temper, but you will admit when you're wrong."

"Doesn't happen often."

"You wish. Besides being cute when you're forced to admit you weren't right, you love vanilla ice cream, books and horror movies, are addicted to soda and chocolate—milk chocolate, not the dark kind—and love your men to be tall, overpowering, and frankly, awesome."

She snickered. "Awesome?"

"Well, I'm smart, funny, handsome, and I can't get enough of you. In what way aren't I awesome for you?" He asked just as they pulled into her driveway. It was dark enough that he could only see her expression in the dash's ambient light.

She watched him with caution, no longer so open, and her guardedness pleased him. Though he wanted her to trust him enough to let him into her heart, he also wanted to be considered interesting enough to be a serious threat.

They sat with the truck running. "Left you speechless with my amazingness, eh?"

"Turn off the truck."

"I was about to." He turned the key and the engine went silent. The moon tucked behind some clouds, and he couldn't see much more than her vague shape next to him.

"You're not coming in."

"Okay then. I'll see you tomor—"

"Not yet." Maya unbuckled her seatbelt.

He sucked in a breath when she leaned close, unbuckled *his* seatbelt, then unfastened his jeans. "What are you doing?" He was proud of his voice not breaking.

"Our date is officially over."

"Yeah, but—"

"No buts." She had him unzipped and his cock out of his pants in a heartbeat.

Cold out of his clothes but so hard he ached, he could only sit there while she toyed with him.

"I can't wrap my hand around your cock." He could hear the smile in her voice. "Have I told you how much I love touching you? You're so thick."

Trying to take charge of the situation, he put a hand over hers, and she squeezed him.

"*Fuck*. Maya, no sex."

"Agreed."

He took his hand away and wanted to cry with frustration when she pulled hers away as well. But he meant it about wanting more from her than sexual gratification, even if she didn't want to hear it. At least she respected his position enough to—

"*Shit.*"

Her mouth over his cockhead was the last thing he knew before thought abandoned him and sensation took over. He leaned his head back against his headrest and let himself feel.

Chapter Nine

Maya needed some control, and she took what she wanted. All Dex's talk—about liking her, knowing things about her, thinking how much his mom would like her—freaked her the hell out. Because his approval now meant something to her, and it shouldn't. There would be no easy walking away from him.

She couldn't put her finger on it, but somehow he'd snuck past her defenses and made her care about him. Tricky, tricky Dex.

Opening her mouth wider, she took more of him in, breathing through her nose so she could accept him to the back of her throat. She'd never been into oral sex as a rule, but with Dex, she wanted nothing more than to taste and touch him.

He had a sexy smell, a musky heat that went straight to her core and aroused the hell out of her. His small grunts and deep moans had her restless. Too bad the moon hadn't reappeared, because she'd love to watch him as she blew him.

He put a hand in her hair, and she worried he'd try to pull

her away. But he didn't. Dex caressed her while she licked and sucked, and she snaked a hand between his legs to put pressure on his balls. "Oh fuck. Baby, you don't have to..."

No, she didn't. She wanted to. That small difference made him more than dangerous.

She moaned around his cock and bobbed over him. He arched into her but didn't shove her head down. He gripped her hair tight while she played, and the moisture at his tip made her suck harder.

"Baby, I'm ready to come. So fucking hard," he said on a breath.

She hollowed her cheeks as she sucked, and his girth made her jaw ache. Another swipe of her tongue against the underside of his cockhead, then the press of her teeth, and he jerked and filled her mouth. Dex was a big man, with a lot to give. Which impressed her even more because he had such delicious control.

Unless dealing with her.

That vulnerability put them on equal ground, because God knew she couldn't keep her hands to herself around him.

"Maya," he sighed. She pulled away and heard him zip up. Before she could scoot back to her side, he kissed her. She wondered if he found it sexy to taste himself on her lips, because she sure as hell liked kissing him after he'd gone down on her.

"Thanks," he said softly. "I'm not sure what I did to deserve that, but thanks."

"You're welcome." She meant it. "Sometimes, Dex, it's not about you. That was for me."

He chuckled. "Oh? You like swallowing me down, is that it?"

"Yes."

He didn't say anything for a moment, then he groaned. "You like torturing me, don't you? You can't tell a man you like blowing him, swallowing him, and expect him not to be hard and aching all the time around you. Damn it, Maya. You're making me crazy."

She grinned. "Good. Because you do the same to me."

"I do?"

"Don't sound so surprised. I don't normally scream when I come."

"Which you haven't yet tonight."

She planted a hand on his chest when he moved closer. "Nope. We can't have sex on your date nights. Your rule."

"Then what the fuck was that?" he growled. "Because I just came down your throat."

"That, my boy, was torture."

He said a few choice words under his breath—but loud enough for her to hear. "Fine. So what now, Miss de Sade?"

"Oh, kinky. But then, you do like tying me up and hurting me oh so good."

His low chuckle made her nipples stand at attention. "Honey, just wait until I'm inside you again. You won't sit for a week."

"Great." She huffed. "I'm already tense thanks to promises of you and your anal wand of love."

He laughed. "Nice. You come up with that yourself?"

"Riley did. And just so you know, I didn't mean to kiss and tell, but I couldn't walk straight after Wednesday. They kind of figured it out." At her words, he laughed harder, and she joined him. "Now if you're done making fun of me, how about a game of Sorry?"

"A board game? You're on. If I win, we up the stakes from golf."

She snorted. "You already finagled honey into our lovemaking—not fucking, so you said. You've tied me up, had me anally, orally, and otherwise. What's left?"

"I win, no condoms. You win, I'll let *you* tie *me* up."

She thought about it. Tying up big bad Dex would be fun. She felt warm just thinking about it. But no rubbers? Condoms were that extra measure of protection she always used with men in addition to the pill. Letting him not wear one seemed too intimate.

"Unless you're afraid you'll lose to me. Again." He just had to rub it in.

"Oh fine. Come on. You're so going down."

"Sounds good, but you've made it pretty clear no more sex." He left the truck, and she followed.

"Very funny. Ha-ha. You know what I mean. I'll have you tied up and at my mercy in no time."

"Oh, my poor, sweet girl. I never lose when it counts."

"You'll lose tonight."

"Honey, either way, I've already won."

While she muddled over that comment, he dragged her with him inside for their game. Despite keeping things nice and easy between them, it about killed her to ignore his hints about naked Twister.

• • •

The following week, Maya still couldn't believe Dex had not only kicked her ass at Sorry, he'd also challenged her and won at rummy. It was like he'd found a lucky penny or something. Annoyed and sexually frustrated, because the blasted man had been avoiding her all week ever since their game, she spent her days working on her next collection and her nights trying to figure him out.

Thus far, they'd gone on a total of six dates. After golf last week, he'd picked her up Monday, Tuesday and Wednesday night for a movie, bowling, and a hike, respectively. Thanksgiving had come and gone, and though they hadn't hooked up, spending time with their respective families, she missed the big lug.

When together, they acted like companionable buddies, talking and laughing. Hell, she *liked* the man. A lot. He always made her laugh. She hadn't even minded that Riley had insisted he come tonight to Movie Night—typically an all-girls event.

Since Ann was busy with Jack, Riley said she wanted someone else there to even out their evening. Privately, Maya thought Riley wanted to feel Dex out, to see if he was serious about being Maya's friend or taking advantage of her.

Finished sculpting for the day, she wiped her hands on a nearby cloth, a smile on her face. Riley might be a pain in her ass, but she always had Maya's back. Maya knew she'd grown concerned about how much time Maya and Dex spent together. Not like Ann, who thought the man farted rainbows because he was "finally seeing how wonderful Maya was".

Ha. Deluded by her own happily ever after, Ann wanted Maya to hook up and fall in love. Bad enough Maya had developed a crush. Her every thought seemed to start and end with Dex lately. What would he like? What was he doing? When would he show up to drive her to Riley's?

Annoyed with her stupid fascination for the man, she cleaned up, throwing on a pair of jeans and a soft, casual sweatshirt. She put her hair up in a ponytail and added some dangly earrings. Standard gear for an easy night out with friends.

Not boyfriend or husband material. Just *friends*.

The doorbell rang just before six. Another thing she tried hard not to like about him—Dex was always on time. Not late or early, but Johnny-on-the-spot when she needed him.

Her phone buzzed as she moved to answer the door. *Hell.* Her father again, nagging to know when she and Dex would be coming over for dinner. Apparently he hadn't forgotten his and Bev's invite.

She stowed her phone in her back pocket and opened the door. Dex took one look at her, lifted her off her feet and kissed her breathless.

Before she knew it, he'd removed her hair tie and had smoothed her hair over her shoulders and breasts.

She swatted his hands. "Hey. No copping a feel." She would have sounded more threatening if she could breathe properly. But that kiss...

He grinned. Wearing an OSU sweatshirt and jeans, he was a man any woman in her right mind would be drooling over. He seemed so kind and generous, and then he'd turn those stormy gray eyes on her and remind her he had a bad habit of being mean when it suited him.

Especially in bed.

"You're gorgeous. But of course, you know that. So I'll just say it would be my pleasure to bend you over the couch and do you before our evening at Riley's. You know, skin to skin." His grin widened when she scowled, knowing what came next. "And yes, Maya, I plan to never, ever, *ever* again wear a condom when I'm inside you. Because I beat the pants off you last week. Twice. Sucker." She tried to punch him in the arm, but he easily dodged aside.

"Rub it in, why don't you?" She shook her fist at him.

"You hungry for me, *darling*?" He pulled her in for another kiss. So playful, so fun. She had a hard time not smiling around him.

"Who said I've been waiting for *you*? Maybe I had my itch scratched by someone else?"

The teasing left his eyes. He grabbed her in his arms and pressed her back against the wall. As if he'd flipped a switch, he set her libido on high. He no doubt saw it, because he kissed her again, this time pinching her nipple through her sweatshirt. When he pulled back, they were both breathing hard.

"You belong to me. Say it."

She scowled because she wanted to say it. Worse, she wanted to believe it. "I don't belong to any—"

He kissed her again, this time grinding his palm between her legs. The door was open behind him. Anyone could walk by and see him molesting her against the wall. But he didn't seem to care. His rough treatment lit her up like a firecracker. After a week of celibacy while dealing with him so tantalizingly near, she was primed to launch.

"Say it," he ordered, his voice deep.

"I…" She tried to move, but he had her firmly against the wall. His palm had found and refused to leave her clit, and she tried to escape her looming orgasm.

"*Say it.*"

"Dex. I'm yours. Oh, oh. *Yes*," she moaned as her body clenched. She trembled through her rushing orgasm, embarrassed that he could manipulate her so easily.

"That's good, baby. Real good." He smiled at her and let her go, catching her when she sagged against the wall. "If it makes you feel any better, I've been telling Selena and her friends that I'm yours."

Her strength returned in a flash. "*What?*"

"Unless I was wrong. I could tell her I'm available after all, that I was mistaken and—"

"Oh shut up. You're mine, I'm yours. Whatever." She stomped around him, grabbing the bottle of wine she'd bought for the evening. "Come on." She grabbed his hand and dragged him outside, then locked up behind her.

She grabbed him by the hand again, holding onto *her* man. "For now," she reminded him, and herself. "We're kind of a couple *for now*. It would look bad if Selena was fooling with you while we're a supposed item."

"Sure, sure."

She hated that he didn't sound like he believed her, and

that she didn't believe herself. She'd fallen for Dexter Black. Now she could only hope she could keep herself apart enough so when he left her, he didn't ruin her for other guys forever.

• • •

Dex enjoyed how flustered Maya seemed as he drove them to Riley's. Maya liked being with him. He knew it. Her denial was cute, but it also hinted at the obstacle he needed to cross. That chip on her shoulder she had when it came to letting anyone get close. Ever since he'd known her, she'd had two best friends—period. Her father was the only other constant in her life.

He wanted it all. Maya in his life. Her love, her laughter, her children. So far, so good. He'd been taking it slow, well, as slow as one could go with a woman as sexy as her. Abstaining from sex for so long had nearly done him in. Bringing her to orgasm just now would have to sustain him until they had some private time together.

Surprisingly enough, his gambit of no sex while dating had paid off. He'd learned so much more about her this past week.

"Why are you so quiet?"

"Why do you sound so suspicious?" he asked, trying not to smile.

"What can I say? I'm not a trusting soul."

"You got that right." He paused. "So when are you going to tell everyone we're dating?"

"They already know that."

"No, they know that I—and I quote—'blackmailed' you into a few excursions."

"Seven if we count tonight."

"We're not counting tonight." It amused him that she kept trying to get out of being with him, hurrying up their time together. If she didn't see him as a threat, she would have ridden out their time with a blah attitude. So far so good. Hell, he'd been invited to movie night. He was nearly *in*. "Look, we're a couple, right? I mean, you aren't fucking anyone else, and I'm not fucking anyone but you. That makes us a couple."

"I guess."

"Don't kill yourself rushing to claim me or anything," he said drily. "If it's that big a deal, I can always call Selena and—"

"Nice try, but I know you can't stand her." She sounded so smug.

"True, but her friends are attractive, and some of them are nice."

Not so smug now. She frowned. "We're a couple. Happy now?"

"I will be at some point, I'm sure." He shifted in his seat. "Getting you off made me hard."

"Everything makes you hard." She smirked.

Her dark hair lay like a glossy mane over her arm. So shiny and black. Her eyes sparkled with mischief, and the flush on her cheeks looked too perfect to be real. "Jesus, Maya. You are without a doubt the most beautiful woman I've ever seen."

Her cheeks turned pinker. "Whatever."

"Now you say thank you. Accept the compliment."

"Thanks," she muttered.

"Look, I don't want to pressure you. If my being with any of Selena's friends bothers you because they're affiliated with Selena, I could always ask Riley out. She's perfect. She's nice and she cooks like a dream."

Her scowl made his entire world brighter. "Leave Riley alone."

"Why? Jealous?"

"Jealous? *Jealous?*"

"You said that already." Was it wrong to have such fun at her expense?

She cleared her throat. "She deserves someone who really loves her."

"Why can't I love her? She's an amazing woman."

Maya sputtered but couldn't come up with anything better than, "We're dating. Leave it at that."

He continued to goad her all the way to Riley's. When he parked, she stormed out of the truck and slammed into her friend's house. It promised to be a fun evening, for sure.

• • •

An hour later, he sat back and patted his stomach. "Riley, marry me."

She laughed, though Maya glared holes through him.

"Relax, Maya. Everyone knows you're my girl." He was getting a huge kick out of reaffirming their relationship in a public setting—assuming one other person could count as public. The more he said it, the more right it felt, and the more nervous she seemed to get. Maya never seemed uncertain about anything, so her nerves around him continued to be a good sign.

Riley winked at him and he upped the wattage of his smile. "I can't help being bowled over by such an amazing meal. Chicken pot pie is like my all-time favorite, and that crust was amazing."

"You already said amazing," Maya sniped.

"Now, Maya, be nice." Riley stood to collect his plate when he tried to get up and take it to the sink. "It's a pleasure to cook for someone who appreciates it."

"Hey. I appreciate it," Maya said.

Riley put their plates in the sink. "You aren't happy

unless I make dessert."

"Did you?" Maya asked.

"Yeah, did you?" Dex echoed.

Riley put her hands on her hips. "Yes, but honestly, wouldn't the pot pie have been enough?"

"Yes," he said at the same time Maya said, "No."

Riley laughed, and Maya excused herself to the bathroom.

Riley sat next to Dex at the table and grabbed his arm. "Okay, what's the deal?"

"The deal?"

The woman had a tight grip. She was going to leave bruises on his forearm. "With you and Maya."

"Truth?"

She nodded.

"I love her. But she's a flight risk, so I'm stepping lightly."

Riley gave him a gorgeous smile. It wasn't hard to tell what his cousin saw in her. What any man would. "Well then."

"Got any tips?"

She glanced at the hallway where Maya had disappeared, and seemed to consider her next words. "She'll try to push you away before you can leave her."

"I won't leave."

"So prove it by staying, no matter what. You haven't bored her, and I think she's falling for you. But that's just my take. It goes without saying, you hurt her, I'll find a way to poison you."

"Ah, okay."

"I mean it. You won't leave the bathroom for a week."

"I believe you."

Riley seemed satisfied. "Look, her mom left her when she was just a kid, and it did a number on her. She acts all confident and tough, but she's really a marshmallow inside. She'll do anything for those she loves. Remember that."

"Thanks, Riley." He took her hand and kissed the back

of it, amused when she seemed flustered. "I'm glad she has friends like you and Ann."

"I always liked you." She smiled at him and gripped his hand in hers. "Your cousin, however…"

Which was how Maya found them when she returned. "What the hell is this?"

Dex stood and twirled Riley in his arms. "Guess what, Maya? Riley agreed to a threesome. I am the happiest man on the planet."

"Ew." Riley shoved at his chest to get free.

Maya tried to hold onto her scowl but couldn't. "You're such a doofus."

"Did I say threesome? I meant foursome. Quick, Riley. Call Ann. Jack'll be cool with it. He owes me."

Riley glared at him. "I think I'm going to throw up. I take back everything I said about you being charming." But he caught the grin she tried to hide.

Maya subtly inserted herself between the two of them, and he saw Riley give him a thumbs-up before Maya turned a suspicious glance her way. "So…"

"So?" he asked.

"My dad wants you to come to dinner."

"Oh, I'm meeting the parents." He grinned. "Should I propose to you there, do you think? Or in private?"

Maya stared at him in shock or horror—maybe a bit of both, he couldn't tell. And he laughed and laughed. She finally relaxed, but he realized he needed to move things along. The next time he asked her about marriage, she needed to be on her knees crying out a *yes*, not looking as if he'd just asked to sleep with her best friend.

Chapter Ten

Maya didn't know how he'd done it, but Dex had charmed her out of her bad mood and turned Riley into a blushing pile of goo in the process. It was like he had some kind of weird effect on women in general. Had she met *anyone* with two X chromosomes who didn't like him?

A few days after movie night at Riley's, they met for date number seven—because he'd refused to count their *last* date as number seven, a point she still had a beef with. As of today, she'd now gone ten days without having sex. She didn't count the orgasm he'd given her Friday, because they hadn't been naked. She was going stark raving mad, her need for him growing by the second.

She counted the time between his calls, and his texts brought warmth to the places inside her that were normally cold. He frustrated the hell out of her, because she wanted more from him than just sex, and even that was out-of-this-world incredible.

God, they really were a couple. He seemed to have no problem with it. Riley and Ann thought Maya was the luckiest girl in the world for having nabbed Dex, and Maya still couldn't be sure how she'd done that or if she really had. He confused her, kept her on her toes and constantly challenged her to meet him halfway.

They spent almost all of their free time together, unless sleeping, and she wanted more. Her nights had become lonely, and not even time spent with her girlfriends filled the void his absence left.

She finished looking over her latest pieces and put them in her damp room for drying. In a few days they'd be ready for firing, then more firing and cooling so she could glaze them. For her upcoming show, she had some pieces she'd already glazed and put into the kiln for one last firing. She had to balance a constant ratio of creativity to output in order to earn a living. Ahead of schedule for once, she felt free to concentrate on Dex. Their seventh date would be spent in his studio, now open for business. He kept nagging her about taking some portraits, and she'd finally agreed to pose for him.

She parked outside his storefront, thankfully after hours. The local police loved nothing better than to ticket anyone who lingered over the two-hour limit during the workday. Muttering under her breath about the tickets she'd accrued over the years, she went to let herself into his studio and found the door locked. The blinds had been tugged down as well, making her wonder if he'd said to meet him at his work or home.

Frowning, she knocked. He opened the door and tugged her inside, then locked it again. "Hey, baby. I'm closed to the public. This is my Maya time." He winked at her, and she relaxed.

"Hey yourself." She walked around, noting the scattered magazines on the table in the front waiting area, the many signatures on his sign-in sheet at the appointment desk. She followed him into the studio, seeing the sectioned-off areas where different props had been used. A large beach ball, a stuffed dinosaur. A dark background, some old-style clothing.

She fingered a woman's lace dress. "What *have* you been up to?"

He saw the garment and laughed. "That belongs to a friend of Anson's. She had her whole family photographed in an old-fashioned wardrobe. It was fun."

She looked around. "You've taken pictures of lions and tigers, been in places like Paris and Russia, taken pictures in war zones. Now you're snapping shots of kids with stuffed animals and families in weird clothing. Isn't this...boring for you?"

He shrugged. "It's different for sure, but I'm happy. This place is mine. I have roots here now. Hell, I have a girlfriend." He winked at her, but she didn't wink back.

"Maya?"

She couldn't put a finger on her unease. "Don't you think you'll get tired of Bend?" *Tired of me?*

His slow smile, when it came, had her heart racing. God he was beautiful, inside and out. "I could never get tired here. You won't let me." He gave her a soft kiss, nothing carnal about it, yet he aroused her nonetheless.

"But, Dex, you—"

"Uh-uh. This is date number seven. I get to shoot you—with a camera, Miss Melodrama. I don't think a bullet would penetrate that hard-ass attitude. Relax already, would you?"

She lost her worry and smiled. "Good to know."

"I want to get these shots right. I left something for you to put on. If you do it right, you get a dinner out of it. I tend to be a little demanding with a camera. I'm just warning you, we could be a while."

"Fine, fine. I respect a man who knows his art."

• • •

"And his subject," Dex murmured, knowing he had to capture her tonight. For his peace of mind, if not his mental well-being. She remained just out of reach, and he had to tug her back. To make his mark before she could drum up some excuse to leave him behind.

She wiggled her brows. "Where's my getup? And just so you know, there'd better not be leather and a whip involved."

"No, that's for later in bed."

She tripped on her way to the back and glared at him over her shoulder. "Funny."

"I left you instructions with your costume." He held in his laughter until she disappeared into the changing room. He moved into the back, where he'd set up his lighting and props. A black silk sheet draped over a red velvet divan. The lighting was soft, romantic, and the candelabra on a table nearby added to the ambience.

When Maya entered wearing a sheer white sleeveless dress that ended at mid-thigh, he suddenly found it hard to swallow. She'd left her hair down, but she wore the turquoise comb he'd left for her, pulling the hair back from the side of her face. She'd applied some makeup as well, and he felt as if he was looking at art come to life. The perfect woman, both seductress and soul mate. And all his.

"No undergarments, eh, Dex? Kinky." She smiled at him.

When she walked, the dress showed off her nipples and thighs. He could see right through the fabric, and he congratulated himself on choosing something that enhanced her skin tone. Fuck, she was gorgeous.

"Good." He had to clear his throat. "Now lay down on the divan."

"Oh, a *divan*. Fancy." She smirked at him, but he couldn't see past the wondrous depths of her eyes. Then he traced her features and was mesmerized by her plump, rose-red lips. She walked with a natural sensuality and reclined on the divan.

He grabbed his camera and started taking pictures so he wouldn't grab her, make short work of that excuse for a dress and slide inside her. He worked hard to ignore the urge to fuck the hell out of her. Ten damn days. God. What had he been thinking?

"Nice." He moved around her, knowing all the right angles to use. "Now stop smiling. Smolder."

"Really?"

"Did I stutter?"

"You're such a pain. Fine."

Her sensual pout worked. *Really* well. He ignored his erection and continued to take pictures. "Now put your arms over your head." Her breasts looked even larger against the sheer dress. The points of her nipples stood out, and the dark shadow of her areolas mesmerized him. "Beautiful. Hold for me."

She did. A natural model, perhaps because she was an artist herself, she did exactly what he said without protest as he continued to shoot. "Now something a little…spicier."

She raised a brow but didn't otherwise move.

"Spread your legs wide. Let me see that pussy."

She blinked at him, then grinned. "Oh. So this was just a ploy to get me down here for sex. Or are you into naked pictures of your models?"

"Nope. Just you." He watched her slowly spread her legs. He kept himself hidden behind the camera when he really wanted to declare how he felt, then make love to her for hours.

She ran her hands up her thighs as he took her photo. Then she toyed with her pussy, and the moisture there enthralled him.

"I'm wet for you, Dex."

His breathing sounded overly loud among the electronic

blips of his camera.

"So hungry for a big cock. Wherever will I find one?" She ran her hands up her belly to her breasts, and he continued to photograph her. "Ever thought about some private videos?"

"Of us together? Hell yeah." He moved closer, zooming in on her breasts. Her pussy. Her mouth. He continued to take pictures, knowing no one but him would ever see these. Art be damned. Maya belonged to him alone.

"Hmm. Want to make a movie now?"

He moved the camera away and stared at her. Like a succubus come to life, she lay there tempting him with each breath. "You'd let me film us?"

"Why not? I'm not embarrassed of my body."

Or much else. "I'm not either." He didn't feel himself putting the camera down until it clunked on a nearby table.

She smiled at him. "Got a tripod?"

"Yeah." He continued to stare at her, taken with her smooth, sexy body.

"Dex, go get it."

He jolted and fetched the tripod. After setting up the camera and noting the angle, he readjusted the field of view until he had her centered.

"Now come here and fuck me."

"On our date?"

"We're boyfriend and girlfriend, now, remember? It's okay to make naughty films."

Christ, but he wanted this. His two loves bound together. Photography and Maya. But this would be breaking a cardinal rule in dealing with the woman.

He stared at her as he removed his clothing.

Her sly grin boasted more than satisfaction at coming out the victor. She looked aroused as well. She toyed with her pussy while she waited, and he noted her heavy breathing and slick fingers.

Finally nude, he moved closer.

"Turn on the camera." She nodded to it.

"You sure?"

"Yeah. Let's get naughty, Dex."

He turned on the camera, excited about what they were going to do. Sure, he'd fiddled with filming a girlfriend once or twice. But in the end, he'd deleted any pictures. None of his exes had interested him enough to keep them.

But Maya... He wanted to make a movie of them together. A reminder of how sexy she could be that he could watch whenever he wanted. The kinky side of him came out in full force when she crawled toward him on the divan, still wearing her short dress while he wore nothing at all.

"Suck me, baby." He stopped at the foot of the divan in repose, wondering how the shot would look. The contrasts of his skin against hers, of her mouth around his cock.

He moaned when she parted her lips and winked up at him. "Get ready."

"Oh, I am." *More than ready.* Steel hard and needing to come inside her, he waited.

She didn't disappoint. She teased him, licking and stroking for the camera. He forgot about being filmed when she took him inside her mouth. She loved him with her lips, her tongue and the sly press of her teeth.

"Shit. Oh fuck, please." He moaned and pumped into her, holding her hair as he moved. He hadn't realized he'd lost control until her soft hands cupped his sac. She rubbed him, and he knew if he didn't pull back he'd come too soon. He withdrew; she pouted.

"Come on, Dex. Let's fuck."

"Lie back. Let me eat that pussy," he growled.

She smiled at him and lay on her back, hiking the dress up to her belly.

"Take it off."

"But the pictures..." she mock protested. At his look, she chuckled and whipped it over her head. "We're making a dirty movie, aren't we?"

"It's a documentary of how to make your girlfriend come," he quipped, amazed he had the fortitude to think while staring at his dream come true. Then, drawn to her, he dropped to his knees between her spread legs and touched her.

He ran his hands over her legs, her belly, her chest. He followed with his mouth, trailing kisses all over her. He centered himself on her breasts, tugging and licking while she squirmed beneath him. "I've dreamed of you here," he whispered and moved back down her belly. "Of licking you, watching you take me inside you."

He continued to kiss her until he came to her slick pussy. He buried his head between her legs and felt her hands clutch his hair. Moaning against her, he licked and sucked while she wrapped her legs around his head and begged him to come.

He put his pinky against her ass and pushed, inserting the tip of one finger in her while two more found her channel and delved deep.

She tightened around him, and he sighed into heaven, licking her while he fucked her with his fingers.

"I'm coming. Oh, Dex."

He licked her clit with a firm tongue, and she broke apart. Her orgasm ripped through her and him while he licked her past the wicked pleasure.

"More, Dex. Let me see you."

He rose on unsteady legs and let her tug him closer. Then her mouth was on him again, and he couldn't do anything but let her take charge. She guided him to turn, and he belatedly realized she wanted the camera to capture them both.

With his hands on her shoulders, he pressed down. "Get on your hands and knees and turn around."

She licked his tip and smiled. "Yes, master."

She turned around on the divan, and he slapped her ass. "Witch."

Her laugh turned into a moan when he knelt to lick her pussy from behind. "So sweet." He straightened and positioned himself to enter her. "No condom, remember. Just me and you."

"Yes. Come in me."

Sweeter words had never been spoken. He gripped her hips and entered her in one swift push. "*Fuck.*" He barely heard her moans as instinct demanded he take her. Own her. He fucked her hard, needing that sweet release to tie them together. In her. His girlfriend. His lover.

He felt her all around him as his rhythm quickened. She cried out when he slammed particularly hard, not with hurt but with excitement. Two more thrusts and the pleasure balled at his spine traveled throughout his body before it exploded.

"Maya. *Yes,*" he shouted, filling her up while pumping to experience that pleasure as long as possible. "So hot." She felt like a glove of ecstasy while she milked him of his seed and stole his ability to reason.

It seemed to last forever.

Then she told him to pull out. "Let the camera see you, baby."

The camera. Shit. He'd just fucked Maya on film. Another fantasy checked off his bucket list. He withdrew, and she turned around and smiled up at him. "You're still hard." She put her mouth over him, tasting herself, and he thought it the most erotic thing in the world.

"You're mine." *I love you.*

She drew her mouth off with a slow lick. "And you're mine."

After a moment spent staring at each other, she shrugged. "Do we turn it off now or go for round two?"

He turned off the camera.

"We'll have to watch that in slow-mo," she said.

He came back to her and sat on the black sheet. "You're a dirty girl, aren't you?" Pulling her onto his lap and wishing he had the stamina to go again, he held her close, loving her caramel curves.

"I am. And you're kinky enough to appreciate it. We just made an adult movie, Dex." Her wicked grin made him sigh. "So are you going to post it online or sell tickets at the local theater?"

"No." He flushed and felt stupid when she laughed. "This is for my personal collection."

Her smile remained. "Oh? You have an extensive porn collection?"

"No, dumbass. This is the first of many Maya pictures I'll have to jack off to when you're busy working."

"Oh. I see. Well, I'll need a copy too. That way when you're busy taking pictures of kids and kittens, I can be home pleasuring myself." She squirmed over his dick. "I'll get all wet and use my toys while watching your big cock. Oh yeah."

"Stop." He held her still. "You're making me hard again. I need a minute."

"I thought you guys needed like half an hour to go again."

"Not with you." He smiled, half-erect. "Hold on." He entered her again, satisfaction filling him because he'd left a huge mess inside her. "Let's get me nice and lubed." At the thought of what he meant to do, his arousal returned in earnest.

She blinked. "Wait. *Lubed?*"

He withdrew and positioned himself at her ass, then pulled her down.

"Go slow, you bastard." She moaned and sank over him, an inch at a time. "You're too big."

"You're just right." After holding himself there to stretch

her, he withdrew, dragged more moisture from between her legs and smeared it over him. Then he pushed inside her ass again. "I blame you for all this. You shouldn't look the way you do if you don't want to be fucked."

"How do I look?" she asked on a sigh as she settled over him fully.

"Like you belong to me."

They didn't speak. They watched each other, and he saw more than she'd probably be comfortable knowing she shared. So open, vulnerable and sexy, Maya watched him without her emotional shields holding her back. He drew her into another orgasm before reaching his own. And he knew that he'd never look at his studio the same way again.

Chapter Eleven

Dex had never felt better in his life. Maya might not realize it yet, but the woman trusted him. She cuddled. She laughed and hugged and kissed him. She no longer pushed him to settle up on his last remaining dates. Anytime he brought up the three they had left, she'd shush him or pretend the time limit didn't exist. It didn't for him, but he had a feeling in her relationship-squirrely mind, she figured when his time ended, they were done.

So far from the truth, but Maya admitting she wanted more was pushing her to acknowledge something she might not be able to handle.

She was *it* for him.

They sat with her father and Bev at her father's home for the dinner they'd been invited to. Little did she know she would be returning the favor this weekend at his own parents'. For some reason, she seemed skittish whenever he mentioned his mother or father, yet he couldn't wait to show her off.

His mother had known of his fascination with all things Maya Werner for years. She'd been the one to keep him up to speed on Maya whenever he asked. And she was dying to see him and Maya finally together, if only so she could shut him up about her.

"You two look happy," Bev commented. She poured them wine before sitting down next to Roy. "Work going well?"

"Terrific. I had the best shots I've ever taken a few days ago."

Maya choked on her drink.

"Oh?" Roy asked.

"Yeah." He gave Maya a smug smile, then described a sunrise shot over the mountains he'd taken—the day after his session with Maya in his studio. "I would have asked your daughter to go with me, but I've seen her before she's had her coffee in the morning. It's not pretty."

She glared at him and took a large sip of wine. "You went out at five. *A. M.* Er, so he told me," she added quickly.

Her father rolled his eyes. "Because you'd *never* spend the night with a man who's not your husband."

"Which she doesn't have," Dex added with an unspoken, *Yet.*

"And never will."

Her father winked at him. "I think someone's protesting a bit much, don't you, Dex?"

Since Monday in his studio, Dex and Maya had spent every night together at her place. Four great nights where they teased, made love, watched TV, played games and just stared at each other. Four days of bliss and torture, because he wanted every day to be that great, but he was afraid if he told her, she might bolt.

Before he could answer her father, Maya said, "Isn't that a bit ironic coming from you? A thirty-year commitment-phobe?"

"Is that even a word?" Dex tried to make light of what

might be a sensitive topic.

"No, she's right," Roy said. "I've been playing around instead of dealing with my feelings. Did it so long it became a habit." He reached for Bev's hand. "Until Bev shook me out of feeling sorry for myself."

"What?" Maya stared at their hands.

Uh-oh. Dex had a feeling Roy had big news to share. Then Maya shocked him by reaching for his hand under the table.

He clutched her, giving her the lifeline she needed. *Thank you, Roy.*

"I know it seems sudden, but sometimes you just know." Roy winked at Bev. "I've asked Bev to marry me, Maya."

"*Holy shit.*"

Bev grinned and accepted the peck on the cheek Roy gave her.

"Congrats, Roy. Bev." Dex smiled at them, inwardly cringing when Maya crushed his hand. "Maya?"

At first she forced a smile and nodded. But as he watched her, he saw her soften as she studied the pair. "You really asked her to marry you?"

"I did."

"Voluntarily? She didn't have a gun pointed at your head or anything?"

Bev chuckled. "She has you pegged."

Roy explained, "Bev put it to me pretty plainly. We're not getting any younger, and what are we doing together? I had a hard time answering at first, because I've never felt this way about anyone besides your mother."

Maya eased up on Dex's hand, but he wouldn't let her pull away. To his surprise, she didn't fight him on it.

Roy continued, "We like the same things. When we argue, we agree she's usually right."

"But only because I am," Bev conceded, and Dex

laughed.

"You want to get married? Why now?" Maya asked. She didn't sound rude. She sounded puzzled and trying to understand.

"Why not now?" Roy shrugged. "I never told you this, but I've been seeing a therapist for a while. It's helped a lot. Living with fear and living in the past isn't healthy." He gave her a pointed look, which Dex inwardly applauded. "It's not good for anyone, especially if you want to find love in your future."

"You sound all Dr. Phil." Maya frowned at him. "You could just date."

"We have been, but Bev is more than a girlfriend. She's my everything."

Dex had no idea how Maya would react, but he hadn't expected to see her tear up. "Maya, you okay?"

She took her hand from his, and this time he let her go. Then she crossed to her father. He stood, and Dex watched in awe as Maya hugged her dad fiercely and cried. She then yanked Bev to her and hugged her too.

"I'm so happy for you guys."

Totally not the reaction Dex would have predicted from her. No inquisition, no swearing, no accusations that Bev might be using her father. Maybe Maya was changing.

Or maybe she was able to accept her dad could find love because she loved Dex.

His heart raced as the fantasy came and went. Just because she wanted her father to be happy didn't mean she was ready to face her own future. Did it?

He heard his name. "What?"

"Well, don't just sit there," Maya said. "Come join our group hug."

He hurried before he missed it, and the inclusion into her special circle meant a lot to him.

The rest of the dinner was a festive affair, but on the ride back to her house, Maya remained quiet.

"You okay?" he asked for what felt like the fifth time.

"Yeah." Same answer, but this time she added, "Still processing what just happened."

He nodded and finished the drive without talking. Once he'd parked, she turned to him. "Would you come in?"

So polite. He nodded and joined her inside, feeling cautious because he didn't know this side of Maya. The woman had never been anything but in-your-face confrontational or assertive. Not quiet and contemplative.

"You okay?" He hugged her, surprised when she hugged him back so hard.

"I guess." She pulled back, and her eyes glistened.

"Maya, honey. Talk to me." He wiped a tear from her thick lashes. More followed. "Maya?"

She smiled. "I'm so happy for my dad. He's been alone for so long. And all because of me."

"What?"

She sighed.

He pulled them to the couch and sat with her in his lap. He held her and offered comfort, hoping she'd explain.

After a few moments, she did. "Winona—my mom—left us when I was three. She didn't want me, and she didn't want Dad. But she might have stayed with him if I'd never been born."

"Maya, no."

"Yes." She nodded. "My mom was full Paiute but not close to her family or tribe. They'd had a falling out before she graduated high school. I guess she'd moved around a lot after that. She met my dad and fell for him in one of her more lucid moments. She did a lot of drugs, and she was a dreamer."

"Must be where you get your creativity."

She shrugged against him and rubbed his chest. "I guess.

My mother didn't want to settle anywhere. Winona once wrote that she was a passing shadow, always drifting. My father loved that about her at first, that wandering soul. She was a writer, you know. A pretty popular poet."

He let her continue, knowing she needed to let it out.

"But when she got pregnant with me, she figured it was time to settle down. She got back in touch with her family. Tried to put down roots. She married Dad after he spent months talking her into it. He can talk anyone into anything."

He smiled against the top of her head. "I like that about him."

"He likes you too. Always has."

His heart thumped beneath her hand.

"But when my mom took my dad back to her family to introduce them, her father wouldn't accept him. Dad's white. Not family, no matter how hard he tried. My grandfather didn't want me either."

"They couldn't all have been that bad."

"No, not all. Her mom—my grandmother—liked Dad, and so did my mom's sisters. But her father was your typical tyrant dad. What he said went. That's pretty much why she left home to begin with." She snuggled into his arms. "To hear Dad tell it, my grandfather would have forgiven her if she hadn't gotten knocked up by a white man. I didn't make things any better when I arrived. One of them, yet not. I'd always be white to them. Which is ironic, because to a lot of folks in Bend, I'm nothing but an 'Indian'."

"I'm confused. Your mom was pregnant with you, and she loved your dad. Why didn't she stay with him?"

"She tried to be with Dad, but she missed her father. And truthfully, she missed her drugs and her writing. Dad made her stop when they learned she was pregnant with me, and I guess her muse needed pot and pills to work. When I arrived, Winona had had enough. She turned against Dad. Against everything, really. Dad was so in love with her, and she shut him out. She left a few months after I was born, then came back, then left again. It went on like that for a few years. She never tried to get custody or anything to take me with her. She just left us."

"Jesus. That sucks."

"Yeah." She sounded so sad. "Dad raised me, but he never forgot her. Unfortunately, I look just like her."

"Then I know why your dad could never forget her. You're gorgeous."

She didn't seem to be hearing him. "He'd tell me stories about her, hell, even *after* she died. Tried to act like she was just confused, that she loved me but the drugs made her crazy. But I read her letters. I knew."

She sniffed, and he hurt for her. "What did they say?" he asked.

"How much she hated how she'd left everything good for him. How I was too needy, too much a burden. She hated coming back to visit. She hated *me*—she wrote that."

"Maya…"

"So all those years, Dad kept himself apart from others. Because of me."

"No. He loves you." Dex knew that to his bones. "He said he was seeing a therapist. He had his own issues."

"Because—"

"Because he fell in love with a woman who didn't love him back. Period. You had nothing to do with it. You know that deep down. Your mom would have left him anyway because your grandfather didn't like your dad."

"Prejudiced old bastard."

He hugged her tight. "Those two missed out on you. Their loss."

She snorted. "Yeah, sure."

"How did she die? A crash, right?"

"Car accident. My grandmother called to let Dad know. According to him, the old woman was beside herself. He tried to visit her once, but they'd already moved. He never heard from any of them again."

Like being rejected all over again, he thought. "So because your dad was hurt, you were too. Is that why you haven't been in a long-term relationship?"

She pulled out of his arms. "I'm with you, aren't I?"

Considering they'd only been together going on three weeks, he didn't think that constituted long term, but maybe to her it did. Before he could even think about how to argue the matter, she kissed him.

She felt hesitant, so unlike his usual lover that he took extra care with her. He gentled his hold, lifting her in his arms and carrying her back to the bedroom.

"Make love to me," she whispered.

He set her down and removed her clothes while she took his off. They tumbled into bed together, and the soft kisses and tender touches grew more intense. He rolled her under him.

"Let me," he said before kissing her again.

She clenched his shoulders and rubbed against him.

Then he was in her, loving her with long strokes. They watched each other as they made love, and he felt their connection as he became a part of her.

She whispered his name as she sought release at the same time he came, filling her with more than his body, but with everything inside him. As they crested fulfillment and caught their breaths, he cradled her to him, bound together.

He kissed her hair and whispered, "You always have me, Maya."

He didn't think she'd heard him. Until she hugged him and kissed his chest.

• • •

Maya woke the next morning awash in a strange mix of embarrassment, affection and unease. Dex had been so understanding, even when she'd gushed and cried like a friggin' baby. Then he'd been so tender with her. Just thinking about it made her want to cry all over again.

She sniffed, alone in bed. On the nightstand she saw a note. A goodbye and a smart-ass comment about how much he wanted to "shoot" her ass again.

She smiled and settled back into bed, smelling Dex on her pillow.

She'd told him her sob story, not expecting much more than some sympathy. A few pats on the back maybe. Dex was a nice guy, after all.

Seeing her dad and Bev so happy had taken her to a great emotional high and low all in the same breath.

Surprisingly, she had a feeling her dad and Bev would make a good match. It didn't hurt that the woman was loaded. That way she wouldn't be marrying her dad for his money. And to know that her father, after nearly thirty years, had it in him to ask a woman to marry him… Who knew a Werner could be so emotionally mature like that?

It made her question where things with Dex might end. Not marriage, though the thought of having him exclusively had a lot of appeal. No. Her father might be ready for a big step like that, but not Maya.

She and Dex had barely been dating. She hadn't even met his family yet. Might never meet them. A well of relief struck her at the thought.

For all that she'd acted like her mother's rejection didn't still sting, it did. A mother was supposed to love her child regardless. The one person in Maya's life who should have given her unconditional love had bailed on her. Maya's father had always been there, but Maya heard the talk. She'd been called a lot of names throughout the years. And though she knew she was physically attractive, some part of her still believed the ugly talk. The half-breed, dirty Indian, not-good-enough mixed-blood bullshit.

Stupid, but she couldn't help it. Prejudice was still alive and well in America. She'd had real-world experience. An ex-boyfriend had slept with her on a dare, later bragging about bagging one more nationality to add to his list. That had hurt, but not as much as one of her old friend's mother's comments. She hadn't wanted her daughter to play with those "dirty redskins".

The worst were the people who said nothing but moved when she sat in a restaurant or stood near them in line. The looks of disgust, the frowns. Mostly from older people. Even a month ago she'd seen censure in an old entitled biddy's eyes. Sure, Maya acted like it didn't matter. And most of the time it didn't. People could be cruel. But she knew more than most that those closest to you did the most damage.

Only Riley—a black woman—and Ann—the new girl in the neighborhood all those years ago—had remained true to her and themselves. They didn't lie. They didn't pretend. She could count on them through everything.

But Dex… He'd always been a sweet guy. Now a sexy man, and one who made her body sing and her heart stutter in confusion. Could she trust him? Should she try to? After all, if her father could bend after thirty years, couldn't she take a chance on a man she'd been falling for?

"If he breaks my heart, I'll break his face," she mumbled, trying to act tougher than she felt. Her eyes watered, and she wondered if her time of the month had come early. Though normally she turned bitchy, not depressed when it hit.

She spent the rest of the day working then arranging to meet the girls for dinner. She sent Dex a text before leaving for Ann's, knowing he didn't mind when she was away for some quality girl time.

To her surprise, she found Jack, Dex and Anson invited to dinner as well.

Jack and Dex she didn't mind. But Anson?

Dex sat at the kitchen counter drinking with his cousin and Jack when she entered. When he spotted her, he left his buddies and joined her at Ann's front door. "Hey, sexy." He kissed her on the lips, right in front of everyone.

The girls smirked, Jack grinned and Anson...glared at her.

Riley also noted his unwelcoming expression and stepped closer to Maya.

"Easy, Riley. I'll handle him," Dex said with a grin. He gave Maya another kiss. "And you. Be nice."

She growled at him, but he laughed and moved back to the guys.

Maya turned and dragged Ann closer. "What the hell? Y chromosomes have invaded our special dinner night?"

"Special?" Ann blinked. "We're having spaghetti."

"*I* think it's special," Riley agreed with Maya. "I didn't have to cook."

"But you brought dessert, right?" Ann sounded anxious.

"Relax. I brought pie."

"Seriously though, what's with all the dick?" Maya nodded to the guys.

Dex must have heard her, because he nearly spit out his drink. "What part about 'nice' did you not understand?" He took another swallow, shaking his head.

"*Big* dick," she corrected, and this time he spit his beer over Anson, who swore.

Riley finally smiled. "Awesome."

"Just following my man's orders to be nice."

Ann smirked. "Told you they were together-together."

She accepted both the disgruntled huff and the ten dollar bill Riley handed her.

"I'm so disappointed in you," Riley said to Maya. "I thought for sure you'd hold out against that square jaw for another week."

"It wasn't the jaw that threw me."

Ann and Riley shared a grin. "*Ah.*"

"No, you idiots." She pulled Ann and Riley aside and summarized her emotional evening from the night before.

Riley sighed. "If you don't want him, I'm calling dibs. Dex is *so* sweet."

"Such a great guy," Ann agreed. "Don't screw this up."

Riley and Ann stared at her.

"What? Why are you acting like if anything happens between us, it'll be *my* fault?"

Ann answered, "If it were Jack and me, things could go either way. Riley or Anson, we'd obviously blame Anson."

"Obviously." Riley nodded. "But Dex is so head over heels for you it isn't funny. He told me so."

Maya paused. "He did? When?"

Riley lowered her voice. "Friday night at dinner. Told me he lo—well, maybe I should let him tell you. And get that 'freaked out' look off your face."

Riley had been about to say *loves*. Maya knew it. Oh God. Now she wanted to simultaneously run to him and away from him. How could she deal with someone who liked her *that* much? Especially because she worried she loved him too? *Capital L* Loved.

"I think she's going to pass out," Riley whispered to Ann, and the pair closed in. "Take her in the back and make her breathe into a paper bag or something."

"Stop. I'm fine." Maya coughed to clear her throat. *Loved.* Oh. My. God. "I'm good. Just, ah, thinking about this weekend's show."

"O-kay." Ann clearly didn't believe her.

"The one in Sisters, right? We'll be there." Riley nodded. Of course she would, because Riley cared.

"Is Dex going?" Ann asked.

"Am I going where?" he said from behind Maya. She jumped.

"Easy, girl."

"I'm not a horse," she snapped but she did settle down.

"Not someone to ride?" he asked, and the guys broke into laughter.

"I see *someone* wants to sleep alone tonight," Ann said loudly.

Jack stopped laughing.

Anson shook his head, still grinning. "I love my cousin. What a funny, funny guy."

Dex rubbed Maya's shoulders, and she leaned back against him, all too aware of his stability and strength. And he loved *her*. "Dex?"

"Yeah?"

She turned to watch him, not sure what she planned to say. "You, uh, I—"

"Time to eat." Riley tugged her out of his arms.

"Right. Yep. Noodles are done." Ann scurried back to the kitchen.

Jack frowned. "The timer says two more minutes."

"Nope. The timer is wrong. I have a hot oven."

"Yeah, but you're using the stovetop."

"Jack?" Ann said. "Shut up."

"Yes, dear." He sighed.

Conscious her girlfriends were trying to save her from saying the wrong thing, Maya let them lead her away. She and Riley set the table, and needing something else to think about, she asked Riley about Anson.

"Apparently Dex wanted him included," Riley explained

under her breath. "The rat got to Ann and sweet-talked her into letting Anson come along."

"Don't worry. I'll protect you." Maya winked.

"I can protect myself, thanks."

"From what?" Anson asked, standing right behind Riley.

"Quit sneaking up on people," Riley said with a glare.

He shrugged. "Not my fault. Ann made me take my shoes off."

They both glanced down at his huge, bare feet. Maya felt bad for Riley, because Anson might be annoying, but no question he was hot. Even his humongous feet looked less Flintstoney and more graceful. He and Dex looked a lot alike, but whereas Dex had a weightlifter look, Anson was more streamlined. Muscular but sleek.

Maya could tell Riley felt uncomfortable, but the girl stood her ground. "Yeah, well, take those big clodhoppers somewhere else. You're crowding me."

He looked like he wanted to say something, glanced at Maya, then sighed and moved to the other side of the table.

They all took their seats and ate. Maya next to Dex. Riley and Anson across the table from each other, and Jack and Ann grinning like fools, making suggestive comments about Dex and Maya that she found amusing, not irritating. Oh man, she had it bad.

Unfortunately for Riley, it seemed Anson felt something for her too.

"Leave him alone," Dex whispered when he followed her stare. "My poor cousin has to handle Riley his own way. Trust me. She dislikes him enough as it is. He doesn't need you heaping onto his troubles."

"Hey."

"For me?" He gripped her hand under the table, reminding her of how he'd been there when she'd needed him.

"Fine. But just for you."

He grinned. "I owe you. I'll make it up to you. I promise."

She couldn't wait.

• • •

An hour later, as everyone readied to leave, Maya finished in the bathroom and had just entered the hallway when she came abreast of Anson.

She walked toward him, expecting him to move, but he stood rooted in the middle of the hallway. "I can go through you or around you. Your choice."

He didn't react, except to say, "Dex likes you."

"Um, okay."

"And I like him. Break his heart, and you'll answer to me."

Fascinating. He sounded threatening, yet he had little inflection in his voice, which had the odd effect of making his warning seem even more real. "Big deal."

Then Anson smiled, and she wanted to take a step back at the predatory gleam in his eyes. "It will be. I know how to hit where it hurts." A deliberate pause. "Math has always been my strong suit. Hurt my cousin, you'll be crying all the way to the poorhouse." He stepped around her and closeted himself in the bathroom.

Huh. For the first time, Maya felt a certain respect for Anson. He might be an ass, but he loved Dex. His devotion to his cousin was an admirable quality. Maybe not enough to wipe out his overbearing arrogance, but still.

She rejoined the others in the living room and decided not to mention Anson's warning to Dex. She was a big girl. She could handle it. Besides, what were the odds *she'd* be the one breaking *his* heart?

Chapter Twelve

Maya frowned, thinking about her boyfriend going AWOL. Thursday night, when he'd said he'd make things up to her, she'd envisioned a night of honey, edible undies and a full-body massage.

Instead, she'd gotten nothing but a smile, a hug and the promise of a sex-filled weekend. Then the bastard had left her to help Anson with a *real* house emergency. That had been two days ago.

This afternoon, staring at the weekend crowd buzzing around the Sisters Art Festival, she felt nothing but frustrated as she sat under her canopy, bundled in a jacket, hat and gloves, while art lovers touched and studied her pottery. The twelve-by-twelve-foot tent housed her shelves and tables full of her art while she sat toward the back with more boxes of her wares.

She'd already sold one load of her vases. Her practical crockery seemed to be selling out as well, and she'd need to replenish after just half a day at the festival. But she refused to be happy about her sales. Blasted Dex had her addicted to his touch. An evening without him left her dissatisfied. Two never-ending sexless nights had been nothing short of hell.

"Hey. How much for this crap? I could use it to store flour," Riley asked with a large grin, holding up a vase with a copper luster.

"For you, four hundred. For the nice people trying to get around you, seventy-five."

Riley moved out of the way and joined Maya in the back, but before they could talk, Maya had to ring up two vases, a set of mugs and four bowls. The rush passed, and Maya turned to see Riley sitting in her chair. "Make yourself comfy."

"I have." Riley stretched out. "Ah, this feels good."

"What? Sitting?"

"Not seeing you-know-who for a whole day. It's like he's always there whenever I turn around anymore."

Maya would have felt bad for the guy, except that the few times they'd actually talked, she left wanting to smack the man. At Ann's house, he'd threatened her not to break his cousin's heart.

So yeah, she respected his loyalty. The way he looked down on everyone? Not so much.

Hard to imagine that he and Dex were related.

"Moping again, huh? Missing Dex?" Riley mocked.

"Hmm. I don't know. Am I missing a man who kisses me, tells me I'm beautiful and calls me his girlfriend with pride?"

Riley sneered. "I really don't like happy people. Ann is bad enough with 'Jack this' and 'Jack that'. Now you're doing it too? Say it ain't so."

"It *is* so. Jack is nice, I guess, but he's no Dex." Then, because Riley deserved it, she added, "And he's certainly no Anson Black, that's for sure."

"You bitch. Why must you taunt me with *that name*?"

Maya laughed. "It amuses me. Isn't it weird that he and Dex are related? Dex is so nice." A word that used to bore her. Now she couldn't imagine living without her personal Boy Scout by her side. Yet just thinking that made her break out in hives. Being happy was like the kiss of death with her and men.

As if she'd summoned him, Dex materialized at her booth and looked around. He whistled. "Nice stuff. How much for the lot?"

A steady stream of potential customers continued to mill about the area, trudging out in the sunny yet cold weather. She tugged Dex back with her and Riley, and they watched the crowd.

"She's been selling like crazy," Riley said.

"Of course she has. Her work is amazing." Dex beamed.

Maya flushed with pride. Stupid to enjoy his approval, but she had to admit she wanted it.

Riley continued, "In fact, I'd say her vases are as beautiful as my lemonade cupcakes are tasty."

"The ones with the toasted coconut icing?" Dex licked his lips, and Maya noted more than one woman look his way. The hussies. "Let's not be hasty. Maya's an artist, but you're a goddess."

Maya narrowed her eyes. "Hey."

"You've had her food. You know I'm right." Dex rubbed his stomach. "Speaking of which, I'm starving."

"Oh? Been working up an appetite with your emergency?"

He shook his head. "I swear it's karma. We had an actual water leak, followed by a small electrical fire up at the house. Been dealing with the landlord for two days."

Riley seemed concerned. "Is everything all right?"

"We're good. The stuff in the garage isn't so pretty. I'm not sure what all Anson had in those cardboard boxes. I don't think I've ever heard him curse like that before."

Riley didn't hide her grin.

"So anyway, I need food."

"Go eat, you monster." Maya patted his flat belly. "Besides, there's not enough room in this tent for Riley's ego and your stomach."

"Ha-ha." He gave her a quick kiss and left.

Riley watched her after he'd gone.

"What now?"

"You love him. Fess up."

"Not the time, Riley." She made a few more sales and could finally appreciate how well she'd done now that she'd seen Dex.

"When is the time? Have you told him yet?"

"No. But he hasn't told me either. Apparently he only talks to *you* about important stuff." Which annoyed her.

"He's probably scared you'll run off. You don't do PDAs much, and you barely tolerate the male of the species."

"Dex is different."

"I know that. You know that. But does he know that?"

"I…" Maya trailed off. She recognized Dex's mother and Selena Thorpe, of all people, standing across from her tent looking at another vendor. "Oh hell."

Riley turned to look with her. "Oh hell is right. Dex's mom and the devil herself? Don't worry. I'm here for you."

"Great. If she pisses us off, you can bean her with a super muffin since you're such a goddess and all."

"Or you could pop her in the face again. But make sure no one's looking this time. We can't afford witnesses."

They laughed. Then Selena and Dex's mom disappeared from sight. Thank God.

Riley left with a promise to return with a hot cocoa. Since Maya needed a caffeine jolt, she let Riley leave with little guilt.

"Maya Werner?" She glanced up from her computer tablet and saw Dex's mother.

"Oh, uh, Mrs. Black?"

Dex had the woman's features, but he must have taken after his father in size.

"Call me Connie," she said with a smile. "My word, I haven't seen you in years. Not since the senior prom."

"Yeah. Hi." Feeling awkward and wanting to put on a good face, Maya forced herself to be at ease. "Nice to see you. Are you enjoying the festival?" A harmless enough topic.

They chatted about art for a while, and Maya felt herself relaxing. A few people pulled her away during their conversation, but each time Connie waved at her to attend to business.

The last time, Connie glanced at her watch. "I'll be back in a little bit. Go see to your customers."

When Riley finally returned, Maya left her friend in charge so she could find Dex. She walked through the maze of artists, seeking her boyfriend.

God, she had a boyfriend. Life was good. Maya frowned. Maybe too good. That karmic cloud hung over her head, and she found herself worrying though she had no cause to.

After looking around the art booths for a bit, she headed toward the meal tents. There she spotted Connie and Selena. Connie stood with her back to Maya, but Selena saw her and smiled. The bitch. Before she could make her presence known, she heard Connie loud and clear.

"I mean, *those* people." Connie shook her head. "I've been coming to this festival for years. The nerve of them thinking they belong here. It's ridiculous. We've had this argument for what feels like forever. Frankly, I'm disgusted. It's bad enough my son thinks he can do whatever he wants with them, but really…"

Selena piped in before Maya could interrupt. "Oh, I agree, Connie. They're everywhere it seems. Hell, I'm looking at one right now." Selena made a face. "And always so tribal. It's ridiculous. They're everywhere, like ants."

"Tribal? Do you mean— Oh, wait, there's Dexter. Honey, over here."

Floored that Connie had been so nice to her face and so nasty behind her back, Maya turned and left. She knew Dex loved his mother, but really. How could he tolerate that kind of prejudice? Was Maya hearing things?

Or maybe he's like-minded and has been playing you this entire time.

She'd been duped before. But never by someone she cared for so much. It was like her father and her mother all over again.

"Oh, there you are." Selena appeared from around a nearby tent and stepped in front of her. "Big bad Maya Werner running from a hater. Poor little Pocahontas." She tittered. "Where are you heading off to? That shit you're trying to pass off as art?"

Maya stopped, ignoring thoughts of Dex's mother for the moment, and considered her enemy. "I don't get it. You're pretty, rich and successfully mowing through any guy with money in the Pacific Northwest. What's your problem with me?"

Selena blinked. "Are you serious? You broke my fucking nose."

"Before that. You've been a bitch to me since third grade. I mean, what's the deal? Did I step on your Malibu Barbie or something?"

"You're pathetic. You don't belong here."

"What? At an arts festival? Um, I'm an artist."

"You're a waste of space. Dirt beneath my feet." Selena glanced down at heels that had no doubt cost more than Maya's entire wardrobe.

"If I'm so beneath you, so not worthy of your time, why do you spend so much of it trying to make my life miserable?"

"Are you kidding? I don't think of you at all." Selena

buffed her nails on her low-cut blouse.

"You know what I think?"

"Do I look like I care?"

"I think you're either jealous or afraid of me. I'm prettier than you. I'm meaner and more successful. Yeah, I don't need to fuck or marry men to get wealthy. I create things people pay to own. What's the last thing someone paid you for, beside an orgasm?"

"You're not prettier than me, you *bitch*." Selena fumed.

"You're just a vain, useless walking vagina. It's flattery to call you a whore. At least those women work for their money." Maya shouldn't have said that, but Selena annoyed the shit out of her. And that conversation with Connie Black. That plain hurt.

Selena's eyes narrowed, and Maya read the woman before she took her first step. Sliding out of the way, Maya dodged the dainty fist aimed clumsily at her face. Then she stuck her foot out so Selena tripped in her stupidly high heels.

"Oh my. Are you okay?" She pretended to lean down to help Selena up and "accidentally" kicked her in the ass.

Selena screeched, but Maya had called for help. "Someone, my friend fell. Can you get help for her?"

She walked away before Selena could make another scene and felt pretty darned proud of herself for being the bigger person. Until she remembered that Dex's mom—the woman he loved like no other—used terms like "those people".

Well, fuck.

Maya had been on the fence about Dex for a while anyway. She might love him. He might love her, though she only had Riley's word for it because the lug had never said anything to Maya about his feelings. Probably best to end things before they really got started. They hadn't been dating that long. She could do without the drama of a guy's parents hating her.

A strange surge of relief overwhelmed her grief. No more waiting for it to be over. She was done.

She returned to Riley, who was giving a customer his change.

"What happened?"

And like that, Maya wanted to cry her eyes out. So she sucked it up and mentioned her altercation with Selena while keeping quiet about Connie Black. She felt embarrassed for Dex—and herself for having had to hear such toxic talk. It made her sad.

She hated sad.

"Maya? What's wrong? Selena get under your skin?"

She blinked and coughed to clear her throat. "I'll tell you later, okay?" Maya locked down her emotions. "Can you do me a favor?"

"Sure. Anything." Riley put an arm around her.

"Can you take over for me here? Just for a little while? I need some space. And if you could tell Dex I'll see him at home on Sunday, I'd appreciate it. I just need to be alone right now."

Riley studied her. "No problem. But call me later, okay?"

"Yeah."

. . .

Maya walked away, and Riley watched, alarmed. That dead look in Maya's eyes hadn't been good. What the hell had Selena done to her? What had Dex done, because Maya didn't seem to want to see him either?

The handsome devil returned with his mother. "Hey, Riley." He glanced around, frowning. "Where's Maya?"

"I have no idea," she said coolly. Dex looked confused, or maybe he'd been caught doing something he shouldn't. "Where's Selena?"

He tensed. "She's here? Hell. I should find Maya before she does something to get herself thrown in jail."

"Selena Thorpe?" Connie said. "I was just talking to her. But you're changing the subject, Dexter."

Riley watched them. Connie seemed irked about something. She poked her son in the chest. "What is wrong with you? I've told you time and time again not to hang around those people. They're criminals."

Riley stared at him, wondering at the flush on his face. "*Those* people?" Had she heard *that* expression more than a few times in her life. Maybe that's why Maya had run away.

Connie nodded. "Those freeloading cart vendors who don't bother getting permits for the festival. They ruin things for everyone, especially for the food trucks. The people who pay end up having to hike their rates to break even, while the interlopers undercut them and steal legitimate business. It's ridiculous to see them here after they've been warned repeatedly to leave. I'm going to have to find David and talk with him about this."

"My mom is one of the benefactors of the festival," Dex said to Riley. "She's a little fiery about the subject."

"You're darned right." Connie glared at him. "Bad enough my own son is frequenting those illegals. Eat a gyro for heaven's sake. It won't kill you."

"But those fish tacos are—ah, you're right. My bad."

"Selena and I were talking and she spotted one of them in the food section, so brazen they don't even keep to the edges of the festival anymore."

"Selena?" Dex frowned. "Why were you talking to her anyway?"

"Her father is also one of the board members. And that girl understands. Said they were tribal and like ants. A bit confusing, but I guess they do organize." Connie nodded.

Didn't Maya say she had gone to look for Dex at the food

vendors, and had run into Selena, who Connie had been...

Riley kicked ass when it came to murder mystery games and now, putting the pieces together, she wanted to bolt after her friend. It sounded as if Connie's comments might have been taken out of context, no doubt helped along by Selena.

"So no idea where Maya might have gone?" Dex asked her again, and she realized his mother watched her with curiosity.

"She was tired," Riley lied. "Felt a little under the weather. She gets over-excited about these events, so I'm filling in. She said she'd be back to see you tomorrow, though."

His face fell. "Oh. Okay. I was going to invite her to dinner with us." He hugged his mom.

Riley smiled at the cute picture they made. "I'm sure she'll be happy to go another time." The two left after buying a few of Maya's high-end pieces, but not fast enough for her liking. The moment they departed, Riley frantically texted Maya to call her, to tell her overemotional friend there had been a misunderstanding. Trust Maya to blow something like this out of proportion.

Ann showed up with Jack in tow, and Riley explained to them what might have happened.

"Oh boy. I was afraid she'd end up in a mess like this."

"Like this?" Jack asked.

Ann nodded. "Maya and Riley have dealt with prejudice for a long time."

Jack sighed. "Bend is a pretty white town. I get you."

"Even though we're lumped in with progressive Portland and Seattle, this place can be a bit redneck," Ann added. "If Maya's scared of where this thing with Dex is going, my bet is she'll pull the plug before he can."

Jack snorted. "Then she's in for a surprise. Dex has been hot for Maya forever. No way in hell he's giving her up over a misunderstanding. And sure as hell not because of Selena 'man-eater' Thorpe."

Riley slumped back in Maya's seat. "I don't suppose you guys would help me watch her stuff, would you?"

"Sure." Jack agreed before Ann could.

"And that's why I love you, Jack." Riley wished she could find someone like Jack, or even Dex. "For Ann, you'd help out her mouthy friend. And by mouthy, I mean Maya."

He smiled. "Of course you do. You're the sexy cook. Maya's mouthy, and Ann's the brainy one."

Ann pouted. "I thought I was sexy."

"You are, honey." Over her head, he mouthed to Riley, *"She can't cook."*

"I heard that."

Riley laughed with them, pleased that at least one of her friends had a happy future mapped out for her. She just prayed Maya read her messages before she ruined the best thing to happen in her life since the three of them had formed the Terrible Trio.

Chapter Thirteen

Maya had thought long and hard about how to break things off with Dex. She ended up deciding on the truth.

When he arrived at her house Sunday evening, she'd already spent a long weekend stressing about his mother, Selena and how to handle this. All that after dealing with the art festival and then the massive teardown packing up her crafts this afternoon.

After entering her house, Dex leaned down to kiss her. She gave him her cheek, and he seemed puzzled. "Maya? You okay? You look terrible."

"Let's talk." No point in beating around the bush.

"Ah, okay." He stood next to her until she pointed at the couch. He sat, but she remained standing, needing the position to boost her self-confidence. Despite Riley's texts and calls to try and convince her she'd been mistaken, Maya knew what she'd heard. It wasn't like she hadn't known an end with Dex was coming anyway. This just forced the issue.

"Dex, it's over."

He blinked up at her.

"We're done."

"Excuse me?"

She swallowed hard, unable to summon another tear after crying all night Saturday and half of the morning. "We had a nice run, and the sex was amazing. But I can't be with a man whose mother is a racist."

Calmly said, maturely pointed out. Not even the real reason they were breaking up, but he couldn't argue against someone sullying her heritage.

"What the hell are you talking about?" He rose, negating her air of superiority.

She moved around the coffee table, putting some space between them. "I overheard your mother and Selena palling around on Saturday. Your mom said some nasty things."

"Like what?" He seemed genuinely confused. "You sure it was my mother?"

"Apparently you shouldn't be hanging out with '*those* people'. Meaning me."

"Those…" He glanced away, then smiled. "Wait, Maya, she was talking about food vendors operating without permits. They have these great fish tacos, and I—"

"I know what I heard, Dex. But you know what? Even if I was mistaken, there's no point in us going any further." Ripping her own heart out word by word. This was worse than she'd anticipated.

His grin faded. "So you're telling me we're breaking up."

"Yes."

"Because…?"

"Your mother isn't enough?" Apparently not, because he just stood there. "We're too different. You're rich. I'm not. You want a girlfriend, and I can barely say the word boyfriend without flinching. I'm not a long-term relationship girl. You know that."

"Uh-huh."

"We've fucked like bunnies, which was great. Really. But I'm done now. I have to get back to my regularly scheduled life, complete with deadlines, friends and family. Frankly, you're a distraction I don't need." *And desperately want.* She should have ended this before it started, because now he was in the bloodstream. It would take forever to get him out.

He stared at her, and she prepared for an emotional confrontation.

Instead he smiled, taking her completely off guard. "The sex *was* amazing, wasn't it?" He chuckled. "Well, we're done then." He shrugged. "I'll let myself out. See you when I see you, I guess. I had fun with you, Maya. Take care." The bastard waved goodbye, still smiling, and left.

She wanted to throw something. Instead, more tears leaked down her face. She tried to convince herself she hated him. But the jackass had been nothing but nice, even at the very end. She cried some more, then moved into her bedroom and tried to sleep off the sad.

When that didn't work, she counted the cracks in her ceiling, each one a wrinkle on Selena Thorpe's smarmy face. She remembered breaking the blonde's nose and replayed the moment in slow motion. But that only made her think of Dex saving her from herself, and she teared up again.

Dex, you jerk. Why did it have to be you who broke the heart I didn't know I still had?

• • •

Dex smiled all the way to Shevlin Park and went on a hike. A long one. The sun had set, and he tripped as much as he walked, but fuck, he wanted to pound something. Namely, Maya's stupid ego for letting pride and fear get in the way of a good thing.

"We're done, my fucking ass." He nearly ripped a sapling

tree out of his way when he stumbled again. Then he felt bad for trying to crush something that hadn't done anything to him and hustled back to his car. By the time he returned to his wet, musty house, Jack and Anson seemed to be in full argument mode.

Great. More tension he didn't need.

He stomped past them up the stairs to his room and slammed the door.

Unfortunately, Anson opened it, and Jack followed.

"What happened?" they asked at the same time.

"Shit." He yanked off his shoes and chucked them at the closet. Then he ripped off his shirt and threw it at the hamper, seeing Maya's sad, stubborn face glaring back at him.

"That good, eh?" Anson must have had a death wish.

"*Why* are you talking to me?" Dex would love a fight. Anything to keep him from rushing back to Maya and shaking some sense into her.

"I knew it. She dumped you, didn't she? I told her not to mess with you. That little—"

"That little *what*?" Dex took a step in Anson's direction, then Jack was there between them.

"Jesus, Dex. Are you eating small children for breakfast or what? Anson, has he gotten bigger since being back?"

"Who knows? Mr. Fat Head spends so much time with his heartbreaker he can't think straight."

"What did you say to her?" he roared.

"Anson, shut up," Jack said. He shoved Dex back. "You too, Dex. Whatever happened, this isn't about Anson. Hell, I'm not even sure it's about you. Ann and Riley were talking, and this seems to be Maya's problem."

"Her problems are my problems," Dex said. "Unfortunately, we're done because apparently my mother is a racist and apart from the amazing sex, I'm an unwelcome distraction."

"Well, there you go." Anson rubbed his hands clean of the discussion. "Move on with your life."

"Fuck you. Why don't you try taking your own advice and leave Riley alone?"

Jack groaned. "Not you too."

"I haven't done anything. I'm building a restaurant. Expanding my career. I'm not the one boning the hot-tempered artist who can't see the truth when it slaps her on the fucking face."

"That's it." Dex flew past Jack and would have nailed Anson in the gut if his cousin hadn't moved. "Quicker than you used to be." Dex took another swing and knocked him to the floor. Hard. "But still predictable."

They wrestled, Dex got in a few jabs that made Anson swear and Jack wince before rolling off his cousin.

Dex lay on the floor and stared at the ceiling, breathing hard. "I owe you."

"Yeah, I think you do," Anson croaked.

Jack stared at the pair of them. "What the hell was that?"

"Dex feels better when he lets off some steam. I took one for the team."

"You two are loony." Jack sat with them and sighed. "When things between Ann and I weren't working, I had to take some time to figure it out, not go all Fight Club. We had some ugly history, nothing like you guys have with Maya or Riley."

Anson frowned. "Why the hell do you two keep pairing me up with Riley? I don't—"

"Save it," Jack and Dex said as one. Jack continued, "But I do know that if she's important, you'll fix it, Dex."

"Of course I'll fix it, dumbass. I just don't know how yet. At least I left with a smile on my face, all happy Dex and hey, Maya, no problem. See you later." He snorted. "She bought it, I think."

"You ask me—" Anson started.

"I didn't." Dex paused. "Okay, what?"

"Do what works best for you. How did you get her to go out with you twelve years ago? Hell, a month ago?"

"Three weeks." But who was counting? Dex blinked, then smiled. "I blackmailed her."

"Right. You've been out with her long enough to have something on her. Force her to listen to you. Hogtie her until she has nowhere to go but into your meaty, stinky arms." Anson grimaced. "You could use a shower."

"I hiked a bit at Shevlin before coming home," Dex said absently.

Jack looked at him. "So you're going to trick her into listening to you?"

"Into admitting she loves me. 'Cause yeah, she does."

"You sure you want to deal with her for the rest of your life?" Anson asked. "You could just date and leave it at that. But…" He sighed at Dex's determined look. "You won't, will you? Hell. You're going to make her family."

"Yep."

"Good luck." Jack started laughing. "You big sap. Ann's sweet. Riley's rational. Maya…" He laughed harder.

This time Dex and Anson joined him. And Dex planned.

• • •

Late Monday afternoon, just as Dex thought he'd figured out how to handle Maya, Selena Thorpe walked in to his studio with two of her girlfriends. God, just what he didn't need.

He pasted on a professional smile. *Damn. Just five more minutes and I'd have been closed for the day.* "Hello, ladies. Something I can do for you?"

Selena smiled. "I'm sure you can help me," she all but purred. "We want some pictures take by a *real* photographer."

She walked around the studio, trailing a scarlet-painted nail over some props. "So quaint. Not what I would have pictured for you, Dex."

"I like it."

She focused on him. "I admit it's…handsome." The smoldering look on her face told him she'd meant the compliment for him and him alone.

Her friends tittered. He recognized the pair as sisters and a complete waste of space. They acted as if they shared a brain and were easily led by a stronger personality. In this case, Selena.

He ignored Selena's blatant come-on. "So did you want individual photos or a group?"

"Both." Selena gestured to the blonde with her. "Shelly wants one with me then a separate one with her sister."

"No problem. Let's go pick a background."

After taking a bunch of shots of Selena, he reset the background for her friends. Grateful Selena didn't hover while he photographed her friends, he concentrated on finishing without fuss and had the ladies join him at the selection counter, where he'd show them the digital pictures they could choose from.

After the siblings had chosen their pictures, Selena leaned close to pick hers. "I'll meet you guys at Townsend's." The tea shop down the street.

"Okay." The women gave a knowing look then left.

Hell.

"So what's this nonsense about you and Maya Werner dating?" Selena spat Maya's name like an epithet.

"You have a face for the camera." Perhaps some flattering honesty would get her to drop questions about his personal life.

She lit up. "I do, don't I? I've always been photogenic." After dithering over her selection, she grabbed him by the wrist when he would have moved away to finish her order.

"Selena?"

"You have large hands. Why, I can barely get my fingers around you. So *thick*." She flicked her nails over his wrist and gave him a thorough once-over.

Only an idiot would have missed her innuendo.

She left Dex cold. He tugged his arm free and left to get her a paper copy of her order. While she paid, he tried to ignore the way she stared at him.

"Werner is trash, Dex. You know it and I know it. But I know pickings are slim in this town." She leaned over the register counter and showed an ample amount of cleavage. If the rumors were true, she'd paid a fortune for her breasts. He could admit she'd gotten her money's worth. Nothing as fine as Maya's but still…

"You're right." He handed her back her credit card and squarely met her gaze. "Pickings *are* slim. Good thing I hooked Maya when I did. She's the most beautiful, talented woman I've ever met." He didn't smile. "Don't you think you've gone far enough, Selena?"

"What are you saying?"

"I'm saying your petty jealousy is ugly. Get over your animosity. Try and be happy without taking others down, why don't you?"

She glared at him. "You're going to be sorry about this."

I'm already sorry I let you in to my studio. He sighed. "Selena, you need to—"

She turned on her heel and stormed out the door.

Dex wondered what Maya would think if she knew Selena had made a move. Despite them being supposedly broken up, he could just see Maya fly-tackling Selena and beating her head against the ground on principle alone.

No. Better not to mention this small incident. To anyone. He went back to plotting, wondering how best to win Maya back.

...

"Can you believe he just smiled and waved goodbye? Like it was no big deal?" Maya yelled Friday night, still infuriated that Dex had left days ago with so little fanfare.

Riley sighed. "Maya, you ended things with him. What did you want him to do?"

"It's been a goddamn week! Not a call, a text, an email, nothing. It's like he got what he wanted and left."

"And what would that be?" Ann asked drily. "I know we keep saying this, but you dumped him, not the other way around. And for your information, his mother is the sweetest woman. Not a racist at all, you drama queen."

"Does it even matter?" Maya paced around Riley's living room, glad Ann hadn't brought Jack to this particular movie night. She froze and pinned Ann with a glare. "What do you know of his mother?"

Ann cleared her throat. "Jack and I had dinner with Dex and his parents the other night… Anson might have stopped by too," she said by way of an apology to Riley.

Riley shrugged. "His family. Not my business."

"It's so weird how he acts normal around Connie and Theo—Dex's parents. I mean, normally Anson is such a pain. But Wednesday night, he was actually sweet and I—"

"*Hello,*" Maya interrupted. "We're talking about me, not Riley and Anson. Ann, why are you cozying up with Dex?"

Ann crossed her arms over her chest. "I'm cozy with Jack. Jack is friends with Dex. Do the math."

"Why are you mad at me?"

"Because you're a moron, maybe?" Riley piped in.

"There's that." Ann nodded. "Look, Maya. Dex is a wonderful person. You dumped him, not the other way around. He's been nothing but nice to you. You told us how he was there for you when you dropped the bomb on him about your mom. He never said a thing to the guys about it. At least, not to Jack."

Riley nodded. "Dex keeps to himself. He's nice. He's kind—your opposite."

"Fuck you."

"Yeah, you're not mean at all," Riley scoffed. "The guy is hot enough to handle himself. You get guys hitting on you all the time. Dex gets girls wanting him. You're a pain. He's sweet. You're a dork about money. He's rich. You're yin and yang. Why are you fighting him so hard?"

Riley's words built until the steam inside Maya needed an outlet. "Because he's *too damn good for me*. He can do better." The last word ended on a crack. "Much better. You said it. He's perfect. So what's keeping him from finding someone better later on?"

"Told you." Ann nodded.

Riley sighed. "I had hoped this wasn't about your low self-esteem."

Maya angrily swiped her cheeks. "I don't have a poor self-image. I'm cocky, remember?"

"To mask that you think you're ugly and stupid."

She glared at Ann. "Hey. I'm fucking gorgeous."

"But stupid." Riley shook her head. "Look, Dex is in love with you. More, you're in love with him. Bottom line, he's not your mom."

"Duh. He's a guy."

Ann's face softened. "Oh, Maya. You've been torn up about your mom forever. As much as you pretend that you don't care, those racist comments always put you in a black mood. Whenever someone says something, it's like you're a kid again and your mom is throwing you away."

"'Cause the bitch did just that," Riley agreed. "But we

picked you up and kept you. You're ours. Do you really think we'll give you back after having had you for over twenty years?"

"That's just stupid." She found a tissue to bow her nose.

"Yeah. It's also stupid to think you should break up with Dex because he's bound to leave you like your mom did. Your dad stuck."

"And I made his life miserable," came out without her meaning it to.

"Maya." Ann patted a spot beside her on the couch.

She took it, and Riley moved to sit on her coffee table so she could see her.

"Your dad loves you like crazy. Heck, if he married someone else when you were ten, would that have made your mom leaving any easier?" Ann sounded so reasonable.

"You make me sound like a dumb kid."

"Right now you *are* a dumb kid," Riley said with a tone Maya wasn't sure she liked. "Do you have any idea what you're throwing away? How much I'd love to have someone look at me the way Dex looks at you? To feel that connection? You sparkle when you're around him."

Maya tried to laugh off the hurt. "It's only been a month."

"That boy dragged you kicking and screaming to his prom twelve years ago." Riley got into her face. "A sweet kid who thought you were his whole world. Now years later, he's a grown man who still thinks you're awesome. So maybe you don't work out later. Maybe you grow apart after ten years and split. Or maybe you live for the next fifty years arguing about who takes out the garbage. At least have the guts to see how things could be."

Was she so afraid of life that she'd made a mess she shouldn't have?

"Look at it this way, Maya," Ann said. "Worst case, you have a broken heart but no regrets. You gave it your all.

You're not a quitter or a coward. You stand up to people all the time. You broke Selena's nose!"

Riley snickered. "That's so classic."

"Why be such a wuss now?" Ann snapped. "Remember our pact? About getting closure? About dealing with the men who wronged us? Except you're the one who wronged Dex. Put it right. If nothing else, at least know you gave him your best. Because all these tears? Being afraid? Is that really your best?"

Maya sighed and leaned back into the couch. "You guys are better than any therapy, ice cream or double fudge brownies a girl could hope to have. You're right."

"Can I quote you on that?" Riley asked. "I don't often hear you admit when we're right. Usually it's just lots of drama, foot stomping and a broken nose or two. But hey, you sound almost rational."

"You know, since I mentioned brownies, I don't suppose you brought any?"

Riley grinned. "Double fudge, because you've been a double bitch lately."

"Funny."

Ann chuckled. "Jack won't come anywhere near me if you're in the vicinity. I've been told in no uncertain terms that until you're sane again, girls' night remain girls' night."

"That's all it takes?" Riley teased. "A little Maya nuttiness? Now we know how to pry you away."

"With a crowbar," Maya added and blew her nose. "We're glad you're in love and all, but you can't bring him to wine night anymore. He ruins a good case of man-mad."

"I concede. No more guys on Wednesdays." Ann nudged Maya. "That means no Dex either."

"If we make up." Now she felt ten times worse. "What if he's already dating someone else? I mean, Selena and her cronies were eyeballing him at the festival and the mini-golf place. He's hot."

"And apparently available." Riley whistled. "Glad it's not my man all sexy and studly and up for grabs. I'd be so worried. He could be married by now…"

"Shut up. So I should go to his place and talk."

"Screw talk. Go rough him up. Sleep with him. Get him invested again. Seriously, I just can't see him getting with some other woman a week after being gaga for you." Riley tapped her chin. "Unless he's so devastated he'll jump into anyone else's pants to heal his wounds."

"He was smiling when he left," Maya snapped, hating that scenario.

"I'm sure he was just masking how much you mean to him," Ann chimed in, then Riley looked at her and she hastily added, "Uh, though Riley made a good point."

"Now I'm feeling bad again." Maya sighed. "I should head home."

"You should. After brownies and our movie."

"Which is?" She's been afraid to ask.

"*Alien*. We wanted to see men die and a woman who kicks alien ass. You're welcome." Riley smiled.

"Okay. Brownies, movie, then home."

"No." Ann shook her head. "Then you go talk to your dad, because you are all kinds of messed up. After you talk to Roy, *then* you see Dex. *Stat*."

"Fine, fine." Maya didn't look forward to talking to her dad, but the girls had a point. Time to bitch up and start acting like she had a pair. She glanced at her friends, now arguing with each other over the merits of double fudge over triple chip, and smiled. "I love you guys. But Ann's right, Riley. Triple chip rules."

Riley flipped her off, then Ann started on Riley again, and they laughed as they argued. Never happier than when getting along…not getting along.

Chapter Fourteen

Maya knocked on her father's door, not sure he'd even be awake at eleven at night.

He answered soon enough. "Maya? Everything all right?" He stepped back to hug her, then pulled her inside and shut the door.

"Sorry to barge in so late, but I needed to talk to you." She paused. "Is Bev here?"

He smiled. "Not tonight. She's visiting one of her sons in Portland this weekend." Her dad wore his Seahawk sweatpants and an old ratty shirt he'd had for years.

"I can't believe you still have that." She pointed to the holes in his yellow Tee.

"Me neither." He chuckled. "Up for some tea or cocoa?"

Outside the wind howled, the promise of snow on the air. "Cocoa, I think. Do you have mini marshmallows?"

"Of course. I'm not a communist."

Her father. She shook her head and followed him into the kitchen. After he put a pan of milk and chocolate on the stove to heat, he turned to her. "So, is this about Bev? Are you okay with us getting married? Be honest."

"I am, Dad. Really." She hugged him, then pulled back to look around. How many nights had they spent talking late at night? How many bonding sessions over chocolate and marshmallows? "Can I ask you something?"

"Sure." He smiled, and to her surprise she saw her own grin reflected in the expression. For so long she'd thought of herself as a carbon copy of her mother, at least as far as her looks went. But she and her dad had the same smile. Imagine that.

"Maya?"

"Why didn't you ever marry before? How do you know that Bev is the one for you? Why now?"

He sighed. "Ah. Time for that talk. This is about Dexter Black, isn't it?"

She flushed. "No. We broke up."

Roy frowned. "Then it's definitely about Dex. What happened?"

"I, well, because I..." She expelled a heavy breath. "I don't know, exactly."

"Did he hurt you, sweetie?"

Her eyes started to burn. "No. If anyone's hurting, it's probably him. I ended things."

"Scared of commitment. I was afraid of that. You can blame me, you know."

"Dad?"

"When I met your mother, I fell in insta-love. You look just like her, and honey, you're beautiful. Your mother had looks and brains, but God, her ability to see the world in a way I never could was captivating. She was like an ethereal creature, her words full of poetry, her heart open to any and everything." He sighed. "Until she talked about her father. You poor girls and your daddy issues. No wonder so many end up working in strip clubs."

She surprised herself by snorting with laughter.

He grinned. "You get yours honestly. I'm an ass and I have a problem committing. Welcome to the club."

"Dad, are you saying *I'm* an ass?"

"Honey, put that shoe on, 'cause it fits." They chuckled. "I love that you stand up for yourself. Not everyone is as nice as Ann and Riley."

"They're not that nice."

"Of course not. That's why you're friends." He stirred the hot chocolate, then poured two mugs and set one in front of her. They moved to the kitchen island and settled in to talk.

"So, Mom?"

He blinked. "Right. I fell hard for your mother. When she started talking to her father again, she changed. That free spirit I loved became weighted with guilt and grief. The old bastard had done a real number on her. That's part of why I never truly blamed her for leaving. She couldn't help it, really. Raised to believe she was better than everyone. White people were the devil, her tribe better than God."

"But how could she be like that? She loved you."

"She did. I don't know. Maybe the drugs did her in too. She was so frail all the time. Filled with a sage way of looking at the world, but she had to toke or shoot up to get there." He shook his head. "Why do you think I was on your ass about drugs and booze your whole life? You don't need to warp your mind to be an artist. But when she lost her muse, her ability to write, it hurt her more than her father's rejection."

Maya thought about that. Her mother had been rejected by her dad, then did the same thing to her own daughter. So cyclical, so sad. *So stupid.* "Do you think she was mad at you for making her stop?"

"Yes. Her father was an enabler. An alcoholic and a mean drunk. He put his family through hell. But she never remembered that part of it. Instead she let him get into her head, let him think I was the one dragging her down. Not you, sweetie. Me. The evil white man." He sighed. "Sad thing was her mother and sisters were so sweet. But they were afraid." He frowned. "You can't give in to fear. If I've taught you anything, it's that."

She took a sip of cocoa and nearly burned her mouth. "The girls think I'm afraid to get my heart broken and that's why I dumped Dex."

"Oh. Well." He flushed, and she stared in surprise. "That blame you can lay at my door too, because I pushed people away for a lot of years. I dated, sure. But no one for longer than a year."

"Try eight months," she corrected. "Amber. Maybe Sherry?"

"Karen, I think." He nodded. "That's embarrassing. I can't remember before Bev." He shook his head. "For a lot of years I was busy raising you. A man has needs, yes, but nothing came before my baby girl." He patted her cheek. "Still my baby girl, even at thirty."

She scowled. "Twenty-nine."

He laughed. "Right. I guess I was scared to get my heart broken again. Your mother did a real number on me."

"I'm sorry, Dad."

He nudged her mug with his own. "Don't be. We learn from our mistakes. I worked my tail off making a nice living for us. You never wanted for toys or friends. Sure, we weren't rich when you were growing up, but honey, we are a far shake from poor."

"We are?" She blinked. "I mean, you are?"

"We—you and I are family, honey. Yes, Bev and I are marrying, but financially we're taking things slow. We've both been burned before." He grinned. "And Maya, she really does have a lot more money than me. We're keeping separate bank accounts."

Maya wondered... "I thought you loved and trusted her."

"I do. But I'm comfortable now. So is she. We want to spend time together being friends and lovers."

"Ew."

"Be happy I have enough life left in me to care. I'm sixty years young. You're not yet thirty. So why are you wasting your time with your old man when you could be hanging out with your boyfriend?"

"We broke up, I told you."

"So un-break up. You know, Dex talked to me a few days ago."

She paused in taking a sip and lowered her mug. "He did?"

Her dad wore a sly grin. "Yep."

"And?"

"That's for me to know. Don't worry, it's nothing earth-shattering. But I got the impression he misses you."

"You did?" she tried for casual but didn't think she'd hit the right note.

"Jesus, Maya. Don't be dense. I raised you better than that." He smacked her in the head.

"Ow, Dad."

"I saw the way that boy looked at you twelve years ago. He had a huge crush on you, and you liked him. I remember how cute you two were at his prom."

"You know he blackmailed me into going with him."

"That just proved he was smart. I *like* that boy." Her dad grinned. "Then he comes back to Bend a success, and who does he target? My baby girl. Why? Because the man has taste. He knows a good thing when he sees it—her. You. Oh, you know what I mean."

"If I'm so great, why did I hurt him?" She felt terrible. "I kept thinking I'm not meant to be so happy. He's so great. So special and genuine. I think I love him, Dad."

Her dad's eyes shone. "About damn time."

"Dad."

"At least you found someone I like. Not a hippy, a biker or an ex-con trying to hide out in the mountains."

She blushed. "Oh…you knew about Kirk?"

"None of them were anything serious, so I didn't say anything. But I see now maybe I should have. You were being like me, pushing people away so you didn't have to worry about them doing it first, hmm?"

"Yeah."

"Oh, honey." He hugged her. "You know how Bev got me?"

"How?"

"I was tired of being alone. Tired of spending the last thirty years afraid of my own shadow when it came to women. Not of the superficial stuff. The parties, the intimacies, the dating. But the quiet times. The closeness. Letting someone in can be awful."

"I know." She missed Dex's laughing eyes, his dimple, those huge biceps he flexed to impress her, as if she needed more than his smile to do that.

"Bev came along at the right time. I'd like to say I'm sorry about how my earlier relationships were handled. But you know, I appreciate Bev now because of the choices I once made. Don't regret what you've done in life. But be smarter than I was. If you want Dexter, go after him. Then if things don't work, at least you tried."

"You sound like Ann and Riley."

"You mean my other daughters?" He smiled. "How's Cheryl, anyway?" Riley's mom. "I haven't talked to her in a while. Had coffee with Ann's dad the other day though."

"Cheryl is still in Italy loving life. A lot more than Riley is at the moment."

"Why's that?"

Like old times, they talked into the night, sharing stories and gossiping like old ladies. Two hours later, neither of them could hide a yawn.

"Sorry, Dad. I'd better go. I have some groveling to do tomorrow with Dex."

"And I have some errands to run and a house to clean before Bev gets back Sunday night."

She kissed him on the cheek. "This won't end when you get married, will it? Our talks?"

"Hell no. You'll always be my girl, Maya. And no wife, and no future husband you might beg to take you back, will ever change that."

"Ah, I don't know about a husband, Dad. I'm just trying to patch up things with my boyfriend. Let's not go too fast."

He chuckled. "Yeah, right. Good luck." He scooted her out the door and shut it behind her, making her wonder exactly what Dex and her father had talked about.

Excited at the thought that Dex might not actually be done with her, that maybe, just maybe, he was waiting for her to come to her senses, she hurried home and went to bed.

• • •

Pounding on her door the following morning woke her. Bleary-eyed, she noted the hour had passed ten. "Need coffee."

More pounding. She threw on a robe, shivering over the cold wooden floor, and hurried to her door. She opened it without thinking.

"Maya." Dex stood there staring down at her. He didn't smile. "We need to talk."

She stepped back when he moved close. Before she knew it he'd entered and stopped in the middle of her living room. He wore a down vest and jeans, and he looked like he'd been up all night.

"Dex?"

"We have a major problem." He ran an unsteady hand through his hair. Totally not the way she'd thought this meeting would go.

"Ah, okay. I was coming to see you later, as a matter of fact."

"Why?" He frowned.

"Why?" It was sounding more and more as if he and her father hadn't shared anything at all about her. No asking her dad for her hand in marriage or begging Roy to tell Maya to come back to him. "Tell me what's wrong."

He looked her over, and she thought she saw hunger in his gaze. But when he met her stare, she saw nothing but worry.

"You're freaking me out. What's up?"

Dex gave a deep sigh. "You remember that little film we made? The one in my studio?"

The blood drained from her face. "Yeah."

"Well, it's missing."

"What do you mean, *missing*?" She stupidly hadn't given it another thought after making the thing. *Dumb, Maya.*

"I mean, I had it at work in the back. I'd meant to destroy it. I'd never use it against you or anything." He turned red.

"I know, Dex." God, her heart hurt seeing him and feeling so distant from him. "I trust you."

He swore. "Too bad I forgot to lock up the drawer I had it in."

"Just tell me already."

"Selena Thorpe and a few friends came in for a photo shoot a few days ago. Selena might be Selena, but money is money. I was taking pictures of her friends when she disappeared. I didn't think anything about it. Hell, I was glad not to have to deal with her looking over my shoulder, if you want the truth. But when I packed up to go home for the day, I remembered our video. It was gone." He looked miserable.

"I couldn't believe she'd have anything to do with it being missing. I mean, I *could*, but how the hell could she know what was on that camera? It could have been a simple theft, right? But who the hell leaves expensive equipment and steals a memory card? So I thought maybe I'd taken the card home and misplaced it. I've been looking everywhere for it."

She felt light-headed.

"Selena called last night. She wants both of us to meet her up on the mountain or it goes viral."

"Oh my God. Are you serious?" Her voice rose. "That bitch is trying to blackmail us?"

"Honestly I don't know what she wants. She told me that you and I had to meet her, alone, in the mountains. I wanted to talk to her in town. I mean, I don't know what she's up to, but we both know she hates you. She insisted on neutral ground, so Jack volunteered his folks' cabin."

"Jack knows?"

"Not about the video. Just that we have a problem."

"Good." Not that she wouldn't brag to her friends about a homemade porn tape at some point in her future, but not now. Not with Selena's grimy hands on it.

"So I need you to get dressed. We have two hours before she gets there."

"Shit. Can I shower?"

He glanced away from her and put his hands in his pockets. "Sure. I'll wait out here, okay?"

After a hurried shower, she put on her clothes: jeans, boots and—in anticipation of snow in the mountains—a sweater and jacket. She'd taken time to dry her hair, but not to do much else.

Once inside his truck, they pulled away toward Mount Bachelor.

The silence became awkward. And then he started to speak, and she wished for that silence to come right back.

Chapter Fifteen

"How've you been?" he asked, his deep voice so familiar and welcoming. Yet the clear weirdness of his tone worried her.

"You okay, Dex?"

"You mean, despite the fact we're heading to the mountain to try and get back our porn tape before it goes worldwide? Yeah, I'm dandy."

She bit her lower lip. "I'm sorry about this."

"You mean about the way you kicked Selena at the festival?" He tightened his hands on the wheel. "Maya, I know she's a bitch, but she has power and money. And now she has our lives in the palm of her hand."

"I don't know that I'd go that far." Maya wasn't a prude, but she cringed every time she thought about Selena seeing something so personal. Seeing Dex naked!

"Yeah, well I would. It was one thing when you punched her. I'd never tell, and you know Anson wouldn't. She had no leg to stand on. But now, with that video of us..." He grew quiet. "She could ruin my life here. No one wants a guy shooting dirty movies to take pictures of his kid and family.

And I sure as hell don't want my parents finding out about it."

"Embarrassed to be seen with me?" she snapped, worried, annoyed and hurt for him. God, she hated Selena Thorpe with every fiber of her being.

"Yes, as a matter of fact," he barked.

She stared at his profile, seeing the angry flush over his cheeks and narrowed eyes. "You are?"

"I don't know about you, but my mother hasn't seen me naked since I wore diapers. I sure as hell don't want her to see me going down on you, okay? Jesus, get a clue."

She felt doubly foolish for doubting him. Especially when he glanced at her with something bordering on disgust.

"You thought I was embarrassed *of you*, didn't you?"

"No."

"Liar." He startled her by pounding the dash. "I am such an asshole for ever thinking we could be together, aren't I?"

"Dex, no."

"You wanted revenge? Well, you got it. I blackmailed you once. No, twice. Now I'm on the other end of it, and I hate it."

"It's not like that." She frowned. "You can't compare yourself to Selena. You never meant any harm."

"Didn't I?"

She sighed. "No. Look, when we were kids you had a crush on me, and in high school I was barely aware of you."

"Thanks so much." He swore under his breath as the snow started coming down. "Yeah, I thought you were hot. And for a beautiful girl, you didn't have that phony attitude a lot of the others did. You were always real. In your own way you were nice to me."

"You made me laugh." She smiled, remembering his antics. "To be honest, I was a little bummed when you transferred to Mountain View High."

"Me too. But they had the courses I wanted. I was obsessed with you back then. And yeah, you could probably say I stalked you a little. Innocent, but I was so into you. I would have done anything for you."

Then, went unspoken.

She coughed. "So, um, you don't think I'm blaming you anymore for that? I enjoyed myself at the prom. I just didn't like how we'd gotten there, but not that we were there, if that makes sense."

"I guess. Then I had to ruin things by showing up in town and doing it all over again, eh?" He snorted with derision. "I'm not as bright as I thought I was."

"Dex, stop." She put a hand on his arm, and he tensed beneath her. "I'm glad you came back, glad you forced me to go out with you." She squeezed. "I like you a lot."

"Could have fooled me." He turned and glared at her. "And for the record, my mother is *not* a bigot. You're the one with the chip on your shoulder about race."

"I know." She sighed. They'd turned off the main drag onto a private road. "Your mom was fine. I have issues, okay?"

"Okay," he said gruffly. "Not saying you aren't entitled. There are some real jackasses around, Selena being one. But damn, Maya. Let it go. You should only care about the people who love you and what they think."

Are you one of them? she wanted to ask. She glanced around at the handsome cabin in the middle of nowhere. So close to the ski resort yet far enough away, tucked on private land. "I don't see her car yet."

"Good. We're here early." He turned off the ignition, but before he could go in, she grabbed his arm.

"Wait, Dex. I have something I need to say."

"Go ahead." He turned to face her, and she stared at him, not sure where to begin.

"I miss you."

He didn't respond, but his jaw clenched.

"I'm so sorry for how I ended things. Your mom was just

an excuse."

"But why?"

Her hand slid down to his and squeezed it tight. He didn't squeeze back, but he didn't pull away either. "This is going to sound stupid, but I was too happy."

After a moment, he pulled his hand away. "You're right. That is stupid."

"Just listen, would you?" So annoying, this man. No wonder she loved him. "You made me so happy. I kept waiting for it all to go bad. I'm not lucky when it comes to love. Actually, I've never been in love." She took a deep breath. "Until you."

"Wait. You're saying you love me, so you broke it off with me."

"I know, stupid." *Such an idiot, Maya.* "I had a big talk with my dad last night. That's why I was so late getting up. We discussed my mom leaving and how it impacted us both. I've been afraid of getting my heart broken for a long time."

His expression seemed to soften. Fingers crossed…

"I got in way deep with you. I didn't mean to. But hell, you're hot and you know it. Don't even pretend you don't know how good-looking you are."

His small grin relieved her. "It's the biceps, right? Chicks dig the biceps."

"No, dork. It's you. You're funny and nice. No, don't frown. Trust me. Nice is good. Nice is great. And if it makes you feel any better, you're not nice in bed *at all*. You turn me on just by breathing."

"Yeah, well, you too." His smile left him. "But I wasn't going to break up with you because of it."

"Look, I already admitted I was an idiot. I fell hard for you, and I couldn't handle it. Then your mom made me extra nervous, because I wanted so much for her to like me. I know how close you and your family are."

"And that mattered to you?"

"Of course it did." She prayed he'd believe her. "You matter to me, Dex. I love you."

Silence.

She kept going. "I wanted more than anything for us to be happy together, but in the back of my mind I always worried you'd leave me. I'm still that little kid who was no good for my mother or the kids at school. Too needy. Too angry. Too white. Too dark. Hell, I'm too everything for most people."

"You weren't for me." His quiet words hurt, because he'd said "weren't"—past tense.

"Why wouldn't I have doubts? You're such a terrific guy, Dex. You have so much to offer. So why would you give yourself to me? What kind of sense does that make?" she finally asked, needing to know. "I'm a grump. I'm too emotional half the time. I have my own way of doing things, and I've been called stubborn."

"I thought controlling, personally."

"Yeah, controlling. Obsessive. Dark. Temperamental. Then you come in, Mr. Boy Scout." She wiped her eyes, annoyed to find herself crying again. "You knocked me off my feet. You wouldn't let me scare you away. Hell, you completely destroyed me in bed, which is no easy task." She sniffed, hoping she wouldn't snot all over the car. "But then you just *let me go*? I called it off, and you said nothing." Her turn to get mad. She poked him in the chest. "How could you smile and leave me?"

She sobbed for real.

Dex just looked at her and shook his head. "Come on. You're ugly when you cry."

"Fuck you." She hiccupped, and when he smiled, she wanted to hurl herself into his arms.

"Let's take this inside, okay? You don't want Selena to see us arguing in here. Or worse, to see you crying."

"Fuck no." She jumped out of the truck before he could help her and hurried up the steps to Jack's cabin. "It's cold out."

"I think fifteen degrees today. Nice, huh?"

He fumbled with the keys and unlocked the door. To her unease, a fireplace had been lit, lights had been turned on, and she smelled something delicious from the kitchen.

"Did we interrupt a family thing or something?" Good Lord, how embarrassing to think Jack's family might be here.

He frowned. "I don't know. Wait here."

He left and she looked around. No doubt about it, it paid to have money. Jack's parents had invested wisely over the years. How nice to see it pay off. The log cabin had a home and hearth feel. Durable yet comfortable furniture in woods and fabrics. A wide stone fireplace that heated the entire living room. A dining table separated the huge living space from the kitchen. Beyond the dining table she saw a long counter, overhead lights, and stainless-steel kitchen appliances.

The knotty oak floors were a smart choice to combat wet snow and dirt and remain intact through the years. An oval rug in front of the couch and another beneath the wooden dining table separated the areas into functional spaces. Dex had disappeared down a long hallway, and she wondered how big the place was. From the outside it looked like a two-story, but she hadn't seen any stairs.

He returned, looking perturbed. Dex removed his jacket and boots, so she did the same. Still confused, but ready to handle whatever came next, she asked, "Well?"

"I don't... You have to see this. Come with me."

She followed him down the hall past a few guest rooms and a bathroom. "Is she here?" she whispered.

"Not exactly."

What the hell did that mean? More than a little nervous, she let him lead her into what must have been the master bedroom. Against a far wall another huge stone fireplace had been lit. The king-size bed had a spindle headboard, upon which she saw what looked like…restraints?

"Dex…?"

A flat-screen TV was mounted above the fireplace, large enough that their home movie could clearly be seen from the bed.

"Oh my God." Her ass was not that big, surely?

He closed the door to the master suite. "Bathroom is through there." He pointed to another doorway near him. "No one in there though. Looks like it's just us."

"And whoever hooked up that camera to the TV." Yep, a camera playing their movie sat on the mantle, plugged into the set via a long cable. She wanted to look away, but the scene had just gotten to the part where she moved to her knees to blow Dex.

"Oh, uh, wow."

He came to stand right behind her, watching in silence.

"Awkward," she said in a small voice, wishing she could turn away. But seeing what they'd done, remembering, and having him so close skyrocketed her arousal.

"Hmm."

She turned in his arms and frowned. "What does that mean?"

The glint in his eyes took her aback. "It means this is only going to be awkward for you." Then he pounced.

• • •

Dex had been doing his level best to set a calm, unthreatening tone. Selena Thorpe? Their movie? The pieces had clicked for him after Selena had stormed off after her session. Blackmail—his go-to and an ingenious ploy to get Maya right where he wanted her. Hell, she'd even confessed to loving him back in the car, and that had been nearly enough to have him come clean.

There was no blackmail. No Selena. No danger to anything but his aching, breaking heart. And if Anson played that fuck-all stupid song one more time, Dex would *break* his cousin in half.

"Let me down!" Maya dangled over his shoulder and thumped his back with enough force to fell a small tree. Man, he loved a strong woman.

"Shut up." He dumped her on the bed and stripped her bare with minimal fuss. So what if his hands strayed while undressing her? Her struggle was halfhearted at best. She leaned into him as much as away from him.

He swallowed a smile. She wanted him back. Her nipples were hard, her pussy slick and smelling of sweet need. He couldn't wait to lick her up, just as soon as he had *his* revenge.

Her right wrist slipped into a fuzzy cuff before she caught on to what he was up to.

"Oh hell, no. If anyone's getting tied up, it's you. You big cheat!"

That earned her a chuckle, to which she responded with some not so nice comments about his parentage, his head, ass, and a few choice things he could do with himself. Yet she made no more attempts to escape. In fact, she moved closer to help him tie her up. He had her in wrist and ankle cuffs, now spread wide for his pleasure. But that coarse language had to go.

"A motherfucker? Really, Maya?" He shook his head and tied a scarf around her mouth to gag her. "More like a Maya-fucker." With a grin, he pointed at the screen. "Look at you blowing me. Oh, wait, there I am doing you from behind. You liked that, didn't you? Creamed all over me."

With casual slowness, he stripped out of his clothes and continued to watch the video. After they finished on screen, he turned and saw the desire bright in her eyes.

"As you've probably figured out, there is no Selena in this scenario."

Her eyes narrowed. So fucking beautiful.

"Yep. I gave you some time, but you weren't moving fast enough for me. Glad to see you came to your senses and talked to your dad, though. I really like Roy. God knows he should be commemorated for dealing with your stubborn ass over the years."

He heard muffled swearing behind the gag.

"You might want to tone down the attitude. I have a ball gag with me." His wide smile turned into laughter once more, especially when she gave him the finger from a cuffed hand. "You sure are feisty. Too bad you let all the fight out of you after *breaking my heart.*"

She quieted and stilled.

"You think I just walked out with a smile and devil-may-care attitude? You just about broke me thinking you didn't love me as much as I loved you. *Love* you, present tense," he corrected. "God knows why, but I can't get you out of my mind. I think about you all the time. Can't sleep, can't eat. You're everything to me. You always have been."

At her surprise, he scowled. "You know, Riley and Ann are right. You are thick as a brick. Hell yeah, I'm in love with you. Damn girl. I made a fortune photographing anything I damn well please around the world. Yet I came home to Bend. To you."

She blinked, and a tear raced over her cheekbone.

"You're fucking gorgeous. Your art is nothing short of brilliant. Yeah, see that piece over there?" He pointed to one of her vases. "I gave that to Jack's mom for letting me borrow the place. She loves it, by the way."

He joined her on the bed and straddled her belly. Her gaze locked on his thick erection. "I've been battling a hard-on since I walked into your house. Been a while since I spilled inside that mouth or pussy." He narrowed his gaze and reached behind him to run a hand between her legs. He drew a bit of moisture from her pussy and rubbed her anus. "Better yet, that ass. You know how much I love fucking your ass."

She squirmed.

"I know. You want it too. Or do you want *me*? I have no problem differentiating the need for you in my life from any other faceless woman. And just so we're clear, like you said in the car, I'm a hot commodity. You have no idea how many women Anson's been throwing at me. I have my pick of dozens."

She didn't like that. Good. He had a feeling she'd find a way to make Anson pay later, Lord love her.

"I also know you've been pining for me. Your dad and I talked, and Riley was a real help. I do love that girl."

He scooted back, leaned down and took her nipple in his mouth. He sucked, tonguing her, then nibbled until her taut bud stood stiff and hard. Her moans for more didn't go unnoticed, so he turned his attention to her other breast. He didn't stop until she was writhing beneath him, and his cock had grown painfully hard.

"Anything to say for yourself?" he asked. When she continued to mutter through the gag, he smiled. "Didn't think so. But I agree. This first time should be all for me. You owe me, after all."

He didn't even pretend not to be excited as he blanketed her body and nudged her pussy with his cock. Her heat had his eyes rolling back in his head, and he closed them so as not to completely give himself away.

Before he could continue, he had to hear from her lips that she was on board.

"I'm going to take the gag away to hear one answer from

you. Yes or no?"

He untied it, and when he shifted, he slipped inside her a fraction. The minx moved under him to take in more. "Well?"

"*Yes,* damn it. When are you going to—hmmph."

He re-tied the gag. "Perfect. Now you just lay there while I take care of this, okay?"

Dex needed her the way a drowning man needed breath. He didn't prepare her or play, but gave her what he knew they *both* needed—a rough ride. With one swift shove, he seated himself fully, loving the tight fit.

She arched up against him, her nipples hard points that scored his chest. He moved faster. Deeper. Harder. Fucking her with the end goal of easing his desire, so he could make hers last all night, he hammered into her, not surprised when she stiffened and clamped down on him, moaning under the gag.

"Oh fuck." He couldn't hold out against his lover coming around him. He cupped her ass and shoved so hard and deep inside her, he felt as if they fused as one. Her body took every shiver and spasm, until he'd emptied himself inside her sweet heat. When his shaking eased, he leaned up over her.

She stared at him, love in her gaze, and he smiled and said, "That was just round one. I'm still pissed off. So I'm afraid it's gonna be a long night. Sorry to break it to you, babe, I'm really not a Boy Scout."

Chapter Sixteen

If Dex thought she would complain, he was as foolish as he was hot. He finally removed her gag, but Maya could do nothing more than lie there and catch her breath.

Dear God, she'd come so hard around him. The cathartic release had eased that burden of guilt and pain inside her as well. Being with him like this, emotionally surrendering to Dex as well as capitulating physically, put everything right with her.

She stared into his dark gray eyes, saw his mouth descend for another kiss and opened up to take him in. He pulled back and smiled, a taunting expression of lust, anger and need.

"I love you, Dex."

If anything, his smile grew more strained. "You're damn right you do. Say it again."

"I love you." Each time felt more freeing, until she wanted to wrap herself around him forever. A little hard to do tied up to the bed, but still.

"Do you know how many times I watched that video?" He nodded to the now black screen above the fireplace and started moving inside her again. Growing harder, not softer. "Every fucking night. While you had a pity party because the world isn't a nice place, I was dying inside."

"And apparently getting off, thanks to me." She smirked, and he shoved hard up in her, causing a moan.

"Mouthy little witch. You have no idea how difficult it is to love you." He put a hand around her throat and squeezed, just enough to constrict a bit of air, but not enough to hurt her.

That dominant pose set her off, and she squeezed him inside her.

"Shit. I felt that," he said on a moan. "You feel so good, and I missed you." He kissed her, mashing his mouth against hers as he robbed her of breath. His fucking became rougher, his cock solid between her legs. In her. "Gonna come again because I have to. Need you so much."

His heavy breaths grew raspier, and he ground against her and gently squeezed her throat, hitting her clit while she grew light-headed from the pleasure—and lack of air.

Before she could say anything, he released her neck and pinched her nipple hard. The pain set her the hell off, because she didn't remember screaming his name, only gasping and trying to catch her breath while her body floated back down from heaven.

He was calling her name as he finished inside her, his orgasm beautiful to watch.

"Oh man," she said. "I love your O face."

He chuckled weakly and leaned up from her on unsteady arms. "You made me weak. Drained me, woman." His kiss, when it came, was soft but sure. "God, Maya, don't you ever leave me again."

"I can't. I'm all tied up."

He snorted. "Smart-ass."

After a while of nuzzling and sighing, he withdrew and

rolled next to her. On his elbow on his side, he stroked her into a hazy euphoria. "You ready to make nice?"

"Whatever you want." She sighed.

"So easy." His low laugh wound around her heart. "Maya, I know this feels sudden, but it's not to me. I've loved you for a long time."

"Oh shut up already. I am so sick of crying," she snarled while he grabbed her a tissue.

He dried her eyes and even helped her blow her nose, which she found both cute and disgusting.

He grinned. "You really are an ugly crier. I wasn't lying before."

"Just kiss me, Poindexter."

He did, then released her from her restraints. "Don't think this means we're done playing. You still owe me for that huge rejection."

"Why do I have the feeling you're going to play this for all it's worth? How rejected could you have been with that big smile on your face? Meanwhile, I was a complete wreck, already missing you."

"Good." His smug grin irked her, and she tickled him until he cried uncle.

"Ticklish. Good to know."

"You?" He leaned closer.

"Guess you'll just have to find out."

. . .

Hours later, as they lay in each other's arms, she conceded Dex to be the winner. "I don't know how you do it, but I can't keep up with you. And that's never happened to me before."

"You're just weak from lack of food." He nudged her with that cock that never seemed to quit. "How about a protein shake? Then I'll get you some of the sticky rolls Riley baked for us."

She perked up. "Those are my favorite."

He smiled. "Honey, I know everything about you. And I still love you."

"A miracle."

"Don't I know it." He nudged her again.

With a put-upon sigh, she scooted down his body as he sat up against the headboard. "The things I do for love."

"Do it fast. You look undernourished." He closed his eyes and moaned her name while she took him between her lips. He'd had her every way possible and then some, yet he wanted her again.

That boosted her confidence like nothing else could. As did his hapless pleas for mercy, which she had no intention of giving. After taking the large man down a peg and swallowing his release, she let him serve her in bed.

They ate decadent pecan sticky rolls by the fire and critiqued their earlier performance on the video. Though she liked what he'd done with the red velvet divan and black silk sheet, she wanted to try that option of leather and a whip next time.

He looked interested. "Oh, some spanking and slapping. How about nipple clamps?"

She grabbed his arm and pulled his hand toward her then licked the sticky frosting from his fingers. As expected, he grew hard. "I can work with that. If you can work with me on something else."

"Anything for you. Two kids, maybe three. A house downtown? No? Maybe Tumalo with a lot of land?"

She started. "I hadn't thought as far as kids yet." But to her surprise, the notion excited her. "I'd like boys."

"I'd like girls." He sighed. "Guess we'll have to try a lot to get what we want."

"Shouldn't be a problem." She circled his cock with a

sticky finger he'd missed. "Oh no. I got you messy again."

"Have to lick it off, I'm afraid." He groaned when she bent down. Grabbing her, he pulled her into him for a hug. "I was kidding. No more. I think my dick is in danger of falling off."

"Yet you're still hard."

"I blame you." He smiled at her. "Seriously though. I want to marry you. I can wait on the kids, but how would you feel about getting married next summer?"

She stared into his eyes. "Gray has got to be my new favorite color." She kissed him, the promise of tomorrow in her touch. "And I love June. I'm in."

He hugged her so tightly she squeaked. When she tried to pull her head back to look at him again, he wouldn't let go. Then she heard him sniff.

"Oh my God. Dex. You're not crying are you?" Her big tough Marine, a man who could bench press her with one hand, crying? "You really are a marshmallow, aren't you?"

"Fuck off, Maya—I love you."

"And there we go. Only *my* man could get away with *fuck off* and *I love you* in the same sentence."

They sat together, lost in that nowhere time of love. Then Maya asked, "So what were you saying before I sidetracked us about kids?"

"Maya Jr. will have me wrapped around her finger in a heartbeat." He smiled and looked down at her, his grin fading.

"Dex?"

"You love me, right?"

"Yes."

"You know I love you. Will do anything for you. I accept the Terrible Trio in its entirety. Your friends are my friends. Your family is my family. And vice versa… So about—"

"Oh man. You're going to mention Anson, aren't you?

While we're naked and in bed?"

"Honey, he's my cousin. More like a brother. He needs help."

"He sure does." She grimaced. "He's insufferable. Arrogant. Too smart and rich for his own good."

"All that. I totally agree." He nodded. "And he's hopeless when it comes to Riley."

"I just knew you were going to go there. No way. Uh-uh."

"Maya, honey. For me. Please?"

She looked into his eyes and melted. "Ugh. What is happening to the tough broad I used to be? Damn it. Fine. I'll help. But only because she's practically my sister, and I know she has a thing for your uppity cousin. By all that's holy though, you have to get him to check that ego."

"I will, I swear."

She blew out a breath. "This won't be easy, you know. Ann and Jack were always a couple. And you always had a thing for me."

"And?"

"Well, I thought you were cute, even as a geek. And as a man, just...wow. You're the whole package, lover."

"Like I said, chicks dig the biceps."

"But this thing with Riley and Anson? That's going to take a lot of work."

"I have faith in us. And in Jack. He's big on hooking Riley up to spare himself the pain of Ann's mandatory couple's nights."

"So we're now doing this for Jack?"

"And out of pity for Anson. Just think how much he'd hate being pitied."

She liked that a lot. "Sounds good. And hey, on the bright side, at least Riley can finally get laid again."

"Um, not to brag or anything, but the Black cousins are hell on wheels between the sheets. You should see the list of women begging to get back into his black book."

"That's a good thing?"

"He's good in bed. He's stable, financially and emotionally. He's loyal to the bone. It's just his attitude we need to work around."

Maya had made up her mind. "Fine. But I'm only doing this for Riley. Who, for the record, will never bake us anything again if she finds out we're conspiring to set her up with her arch nemesis."

"Hey, I don't plan on screwing up a good thing. Think she'd bake us another batch of sticky rolls if I tell her how terrible Anson is for moving right next to her shop?"

"Totally. Let's get dressed."

He stopped her with another hug. "Let's not. We still have a few positions I haven't been able to try with you yet. And we have this big old bed and these perfectly fashioned cuffs..."

Maya laughed. "You're on, Boy Scout. Now why don't you help this little old lady to the edge of the bed. She needs help finding something long and thick to ride."

"Save a horse, ride a Marine?"

"Ooo fucking rah."

He laughed. "I love you."

About the Author

Caffeine addict, boy referee, and romance aficionado, NY Times and *USA Today* bestselling author Marie Harte has over 100 books published with more constantly on the way. She's a confessed bibliophile and devotee of action movies. Whether hiking in Central Oregon, biking around town, or hanging at the local tea shop, she's constantly plotting to give everyone a happily ever after. Visit http://marieharte.com and fall in love.

You can contact her at marie_harte@yahoo.com.

Enjoy the entire Best Revenge series…

SERVED COLD

SERVED HOT

SERVED SWEET

If you love sexy romance, one-click these steamy Brazen releases…

ONE WEEK WITH THE MARINE
a *Love on Location* novel by Alison Gatta

Avery Forrester has never been the type to settle down. Still, when U.S. Marine Holden Morris, her long-term best friend with benefits, comes home on leave with a plan—including marriage and children—she realizes she'll have to do something drastic in order to keep him. Luckily, drastic is what she does best.

RENEGADE
a *Phoenix Rising* novel by Brynley Blake

All photographer Gemma Ward wants is a man who can handle her. She thinks she's found her guy, but she needs to convince him she has some experience in his singularly erotic lifestyle. Luckily, her best friend Walker Kincaid shows up and reluctantly offers to help her. But it isn't long before those lessons in pleasure turn into a whole lot more…

Leveling the Field
a *Gamers* novel by Megan Erickson

Reclusive gaming magazine exec Ethan Talley is furious when his business partner hires a photographer—a *gorgeous* photographer with an affinity for glitter and sex—to take pictures for the newspaper. No matter how badly he wants the woman…under him, over him, against the nearest wall…he has reasons for not wanting to be on camera anymore, and his scars are only one of them.

Hold Me Until Morning
a *Grayson Brothers* novel by Christina Phillips

Cooper Grayson is supposed to hole up in a mountain cabin and protect his best friend's little sister from the paparazzi for a week. That's it. But Paris O'Connell isn't a kid anymore, and when they finally kiss, Cooper leaves her bare. Exposed. His for the taking. And take he does. But when the real world crashes in, so does reality. And reality tells them there's no way a Hollywood star and a bad boy from the wrong side of town could ever have a future together…